DOCTOR WHO

BBC CHILDREN'S BOOKS

UK | USA | Canada | Ireland | Australia
India | New Zealand | South Africa

BBC Children's Books are published by Puffin Books,
part of the Penguin Random House group of companies
whose addresses can be found at global.penguinrandomhouse.com

www.penguin.co.uk
www.puffin.co.uk
www.ladybird.co.uk

First published by Puffin Books 2012
This edition first published by Puffin Books 2016

001

Written by Richard Dungworth
Copyright © BBC Worldwide Limited, 2016

BBC, DOCTOR WHO (word marks, logos and devices),
TARDIS, DALEKS, CYBERMAN and K-9 (word marks and devices) are
trademarks of the British Broadcasting Corporation and are used under licence.
BBC logo © BBC, 1996. Doctor Who logo © BBC, 2009

Printed in Great Britain by Clays Ltd, St Ives plc

A CIP catalogue record for this book is available from the British Library

ISBN: 978-1-405-92254-8

All correspondence to:
BBC Children's Books
Penguin Random House Children's
80 Strand, London WC2R 0RL

Penguin Random House is committed to a
sustainable future for our business, our readers
and our planet. This book is made from Forest
Stewardship Council® certified paper.

BBC
DOCTOR WHO
EXTRA TIME

Richard Dungworth

PUFFIN

Contents

Chapter 1

On the Beat

Police Constable Sanderson was feeling rather sorry
for himself.

He stood on the corner of Fulton Road and
watched the parade of excited football fans
pass noisily by. A steady stream of people moved
south along the straight, broad route of Olympic Way,
and others were making their way from Wembley
Park Underground station, or spilling out of bright
red double-decker buses on to Fulton Road and
joining the flow. It was as if everyone in north-west
London was being drawn to the same spot by an
irresistible force.

Everyone except me, thought PC Sanderson glumly.

The disappointed policeman knew only too well
where the crowd was heading: Olympic Way led
directly to the main entrance of Wembley Stadium,

the home of football. And today, for the first time ever, the scene of the FIFA World Cup Final.

There was little doubt which team most fans had come to support. Saint George's cross and the Union Jack were everywhere PC Sanderson looked – on flags, banners, clothing and faces. The air was full of patriotic chanting, excited chatter and the *tatta-tatta-tatta* of the fans' wooden football rattles. English men, women and children of all ages and backgrounds had come together to cheer on their heroes of the hour.

The young constable had seen big Wembley crowds before – he had once been on duty on FA Cup Final day – but he had never seen anything quite like this. Then again, there had never been a match quite like this, either. A World Cup Final, at Wembley, with the home side contending for the trophy. It was the stuff of every England fan's dreams.

PC Sanderson was going to miss the whole thing. *Trust my rotten luck*, he thought. *Only I would get the Saturday shift today of all days . . .*

He gave a weary sigh as yet more excited England fans flooded past him. Right now the rest of his family would be gathered in his neighbour's front room, watching the pre-match build-up, while here *he* was, stuck on the beat – and not due to clock off until several hours after the final whistle.

Maybe a cuppa would lift his spirits. It was a sunny July afternoon and, under his black bobby's hat and uniform, Sanderson was feeling the heat. A nice cup of tea on a summer's day could be surprisingly thirst-quenching.

He turned away from the flow of fans and began to stroll back towards the junction with Albion Way and the police call box where he had stashed his thermos flask. It was common practice for Met officers on the beat to use the nearest call box as a base; the direct phone line to the local station gave an on-duty officer a useful link with headquarters. The dark blue wardrobe-like boxes had been introduced to London's streets a little over thirty years ago, and there were now over 600 dotted around the city – including the one on Albion Way.

'Do you reckon the lads can win it for us, officer?'

Sanderson broke his stride at the sound of the familiar cheerful voice. Syd Marlin, a newspaper seller and Fulton Road regular, was hailing the constable from his stand on the opposite side of the street. At least *someone* else was working, then.

Sanderson crossed the road; Syd was always up for a chat.

'They'll have their work cut out, Syd, that's for sure,' the policeman said as he approached the news stand. 'The Germans have some quality players. Beckenbauer, Seeler, Emmerich – they all know how to put the ball in the net. But I'd like to think we'll give 'em a game.'

'Never thought we'd make it this far, meself,' said Syd. 'What with young Jimmy Greaves out injured an' all. Thought Portugal would do for us in the semi. But Ramsey's turning out to be quite some manager, ain't 'e? Played a blinder so far. And there ain't a better number nine in the world than Charlton, by my reckoning.'

'We've got the talent, all right,' agreed Sanderson. 'Let's hope Lady Luck is on our side. I guess we just have to keep faith, eh, Syd?'

PC Sanderson stepped off the pavement briefly to allow a party of young men and women to pass by. They, too, were heading for Olympic Way, and all were dressed in the very latest fashions.

Syd watched the group of youngsters move off along the street. He shook his head and tutted. 'Look at 'em, officer,' he muttered. 'Right bunch of peacocks, these young 'uns, ain't they? My missus don't approve of them new "miniskirts". Says they're not decent.'

Sanderson raised his eyebrows beneath his police helmet. 'Well, they're certainly all the rage this summer, that's for sure,' he said.

Syd nodded. 'True. There was a real pretty redhead along just a minute ago wearing one,' he said. 'Stopped off to buy a paper, she did – or rather, one of the two blokes with her did.' He hesitated, frowning. 'Funniest thing, though – not one of the three of 'em seemed to have the faintest idea 'ow to pay for it.' He shook his head again. 'Not a clue.'

PC Sanderson gave the vendor a puzzled look. 'How d'you mean, Syd?'

'Just what I say – they didn't know 'ow to pay. The one who wanted the paper took out a handful of coins and just stared at 'em, like 'e 'ad no idea what ones to give me. 'Is mate wanted a few of them penny bubblegum specials –' he pointed at a cardboard tray of sweets at one side of his stand that had green, black and white wrappers that bore the words BAZOOKA WORLD CUP FOOTBALLERS – 'with three of 'em, and the paper, it came to sixpence. But when I asked the fella with the money for a tanner 'e jus' looked at me like I was talking gibberish. Then 'e gave me a whole half crown – five times what 'e owed! And 'e wouldn't have anything back from me – though I tried to give 'im 'is change, I swear.'

'Foreigners, maybe?' suggested Sanderson.

'That's what I thought,' replied Syd. 'But both blokes spoke to me in the Queen's English. And the girl was Scottish, clear as day, which is 'ardly proper foreign . . .'

A transistor radio – the small, portable type that almost everyone seemed to own these days – stood on a shelf at the back of Syd's news stand. A recent Beatles hit had been playing in the background, but now a new track began with a burst of raucous, angry-sounding vocals. It was The Who, blaring out their hit 'My Generation'. Syd reached for the radio's tuning dial and cut the up-and-coming band off.

'That's enough of that racket. I don't make much of this stuff the kids are all listening to now. Mods, they call 'emselves, don't they? Not enough tune for my liking. I know it's "in", of course, but I never was one for all that fashion malarkey.'

PC Sanderson smiled. 'Nor me, Syd.'

'My eldest is *right* into it, though,' Syd went on. He twiddled the radio's tuning dial again, trying to pick up another station. 'Got 'imself one of them Italian motor scooters, an' everythin'. Wing mirrors all over the thing . . .'

Suddenly the crackle of static on the radio was replaced by the sound of a well-spoken male voice:

' . . . *and the stands here at Wembley are rapidly filling with England's expectant supporters. The atmosphere is truly electric. One can only wonder how Alf Ramsey's players are feeling at this moment, as they prepare themselves in the south-side changing rooms for this historic encounter . . .'*

'Not long till kick-off now,' said Syd. 'I'd best get a move on. Me sister's old man managed to pick up a second-hand televisual set on the cheap. I'm off to watch the match at 'er place. How about you, officer? I guess you're knocking off, too?'

'Afraid not, Syd. I was just going to grab a cuppa. I'm on duty all afternoon – more's the pity.'

The newspaper seller looked horrified. 'No! You're missing the match?' he hissed. 'A game like this only comes round once in a lifetime – if you're lucky. It ain't right to miss it!'

'I know, Syd. I can't pretend I'm happy about it.'

Syd frowned. He appeared to think hard about something for a few moments.

'Here.' He presented the still-chattering wireless to PC Sanderson. 'You take this, my friend. You can tuck it away in that police box of yours. Have yourself a little listen to how Ramsey's lads are getting on.'

Sanderson shook his head. 'That's very good of you, Syd, but I can't,' he said regretfully. 'Not when I'm supposed to be on duty.'

'Who's to know?' pressed Syd, still holding out the radio. 'You can give it me back next time I see you.'

The constable dithered.

'Go on with yer! It's the World Cup Final, for Pete's sake! I'll not tell a soul.'

Sanderson gave a sigh. 'Ah, why not? You're right – it might not come round again for a while, eh?' He took the wireless and tucked it under his arm. 'Thanks, Syd. You're a gent.'

Syd grinned. 'No problem, officer. Now, I best shut up shop or I'll miss the start meself.'

PC Sanderson gave another nod of thanks. Then, leaving Syd to close up his news stand, he set off along the pavement once again. This time, there was real purpose in his stride.

A hundred paces or so brought him to the junction with Albion Way. He turned the corner briskly – and came to an abrupt halt.

Now that was odd. *Very* odd.

It was only just over an hour since Sanderson had last called at the Albion Way box, to park his police motorcycle beside it, and drop off his flask. But within that time there had been a very obvious change on Albion Way: there were now *two* police boxes.

They stood right next to one another and were more or less identical.

PC Sanderson was baffled. The second box must somehow have been put in position during the last hour. But how? And, more to the point, *why*? There were no plans to replace the existing box, as far as he was aware. Certainly nothing had been mentioned at the station. Besides, the newly arrived box looked in worse condition, if anything, than the original one.

The obvious thing to do was to phone in and find out what was going on. But Sanderson found himself hesitating. He looked down at Syd's radio, which was tucked under his arm. Now that he had a chance to enjoy at least some of the England versus West Germany game, he was reluctant to draw attention to himself for the next couple of hours.

There would be plenty of time to sort out whatever the muddle was afterwards.

Having made up his mind, he opened the door of the familiar police box, stepped inside and closed it behind him.

Chapter 2

The Road to Wembley

'Yessss! Brilliant!' said Rory. 'I got Gordon Banks!'

Rory, Amy and the Doctor were being swept along Olympic Way by the tide of people heading for Wembley. As they walked, Rory was investigating his packet of World Cup bubblegum. He had unwrapped the gum, popped it in his mouth, and was now admiring the sticker that had come with it. It showed a dark-haired man in a yellow goalkeeper's shirt. The badge over his heart bore the three lions of England.

Back home in his own era, Rory was a keen collector of Match Attax footballer cards. He knew they were really meant for kids, but Amy had once bought him a pack as a joke, and that was it – he had caught the collecting bug. He now owned an impressive set of twenty-first century Premier League stars, and the chance to get his hands on an original Bazooka player sticker from the '66 World Cup had been too good to miss. He examined the sticker happily, then looked up at Amy.

'Who did you get?'

'The lovely Norbert "Nobby" Stiles,' replied Amy, holding up her sticker to show him. 'Has a one-in-a-million smile, doesn't he?'

The sticker showed a cheery-looking player in a white England shirt, who was missing most of his front teeth.

Rory laughed. 'He might need a little dental work, but he's a fantastic player. Toughest tackler we have – or had, I mean. How about you, Doctor?'

'Hmm? What's that?' As he loped along, the Doctor was browsing the newspaper he had just bought. He looked up distractedly.

Rory waved his sticker. 'Which player did you get?'

'Ah! Right!' said the Doctor. He rolled up his newspaper and slipped it into the left-hand pocket of his tweed jacket. Then he delved into his other jacket pocket for his own penny gum. He unwrapped it, examined the enclosed sticker and pulled a face.

'Some chap called Geoff Hurst. Likely-looking fellow. Anyone know if he's any good?'

Rory looked at the Doctor as though he had just asked if the South Pole was at all chilly.

'Not bad, yeah,' he said enviously. 'Just the only player ever to get a hat-trick in a World Cup Final, that's all!'

'*Really?*' said the Doctor. 'A hat-trick, eh? In the final? Excellent!' He regarded the sticker cheerfully for a few seconds, then looked enquiringly at Rory once more. 'And what exactly is a hat-trick, again?'

Rory was about to reply when he noticed the twinkle in the Doctor's eye – he was having Rory on.

The Doctor grinned. 'I might not have your encyclopedic knowledge of football trivia, Rory, but I do know a *bit* about the beautiful game,' he said. 'Even played a match or two myself, would you believe. I remember one in particular, when I was standing in for my flatmate –'

'Nuh-uh!' interrupted Amy, shaking her head. 'Hold it right there, boys! No footballing stories allowed,' she said firmly. 'None. Of any kind. It's bad enough that I let Rory talk me into this trip. I'm about to spend ninety minutes watching a bunch of men in frankly *very* unflattering shorts run about after a pig's bladder. I *really* don't need to put up with any macho sports chat from you two on top of that.'

'It'll be a hundred and twenty minutes, actually,' muttered Rory timidly. 'It goes to extra time.'

Amy let out a weary groan.

'Though I think they'll have *slightly* more advanced equipment than you give them credit for, Pond,' added the Doctor. 'Pig's-bladder balls were more your nineteenth century. Anyway, I thought you quite liked football.'

'I quite like *footballers*,' Amy corrected him. 'Young, handsome, super-fit, twenty-first-century ones. Not middle-aged ones with comb-over hairstyles.' She looked at her picture-card again. 'I mean, Nobby here isn't exactly David Beckham, is he?'

Rory gave her a despairing look.

'It's how you play that matters, Amy, not what you look like.'

'Not if you want to win the coveted "Pond Man of the Match" award, it isn't,' replied Amy.

Rory looked a little hurt. Amy looped her arm through his.

'Don't fret, petal,' she said, grinning. 'I'm not really the WAG type. Much happier with a nice ordinary fella than some fathead with a Ferrari and too much hair gel.'

Rory's expression brightened.

'Although they do *pay* footballers rather better . . .' Amy teased.

'Not now, they don't,' replied Rory. 'Players weren't nearly as spoiled back in the day – even when they got picked for their country. I saw an interview with one of our sixty-six squad once. He said they had to bring their own *towels* to the final!'

'And of course whatever pay they do get will be in that old money,' added the Doctor. 'Which is *utterly* baffling.'

Rory smiled at the Doctor. 'I noticed you had a tough time paying that newspaper guy.'

The Doctor looked worried.

'Do you think I gave him enough? I'd hate to have swindled him. Seemed very nice. But he said "sixpence", then asked for a "tanner". Hadn't a clue what I was supposed to hand over!'

Amy smirked.

'What are you saying, Doctor? That your big old Time Lord brain can keep the TARDIS ticking over but can't cope with pounds, shillings and pence?'

The Doctor blew out his cheeks. 'Absolutely! Give me a time–space dimensional algorithm any day of the week! All this "half a sovereign, three shillings and sixpence" business is *terribly* confusing! So many different coins! Guineas and farthings and threepenny bits. Last time I was here, someone asked me for "two bob". Bob? Does that sound like money to you? It sounds like something you're supposed to *do*, or someone you know.' He shook his head despairingly. 'Still, it could be worse, I suppose. On Mafooz Minor they use different-sized pellets of swamp-vole dung as currency. That's complicated *and* smelly.'

At that moment, a group of young fans jogged past them, clattering their wooden football rattles enthusiastically.

'Those things make a fair old racket, don't they?' said Amy.

Rory's expression became rather glum again.

'I could have topped that easily,' he said sulkily, 'if it wasn't for a certain person not far away.' He cast an accusing look at Amy.

'Oh, not *this* again,' Amy groaned. 'It was just a plastic trumpet, Rory. It's gone. Get over it!'

'It wasn't *just* anything,' grumbled Rory. 'It was a proper 2010 World Cup vuvuzela. One of the lads brought it back from South Africa. I was going to be the only person in the crowd with one.'

'Precisely!' Amy snapped back. 'Showing yet again how you spectacularly fail to grasp even the basics of time travel, you clot. Rule Number One – try *not* to stand out.'

'She has a point, Rory,' agreed the Doctor. 'That vuvu-wailer whatsit of yours would have looked very out of place – or time, rather. As Pond says, it's generally a good idea to avoid drawing attention to ourselves.'

Rory gave a snort. 'Oh, right. Of course. Like *you* normally do, you mean?'

The Doctor chose to ignore this. 'On top of which,' he continued instead, 'it was proving very hard to concentrate on locking the TARDIS on to this precise dateline with you making a sound like a flatulent Zarusian Blubberhog.'

'She still didn't have to snap it in half,' said Rory sulkily.

'Oh, I *so* did!' contradicted Amy. 'It was either that or your neck. The noise was driving me mad.'

'I was practising,' protested Rory. 'They're really hard to blow.'

'You were doing my head in,' Amy corrected him. '*That's* what you were doing.'

'Now, now, children,' smiled the Doctor. 'Let's not squabble. After all, Rory, this was your dream destination, remember? And we're here, aren't we?

Bang on target. Right place, right time. You're about to get your wish of watching England win the World Cup. I'd have thought you'd be chuffed to bits – toy trumpet or no.'

'It wasn't a toy trumpet!' protested Rory. 'It was a proper vuvu–'

'And unless I'm much mistaken,' continued the Doctor, 'those are the twin towers of the Empire Stadium just up ahead!'

The domed tops of two white towers had just come into view over the heads of the people in front of them. Moments later, the trio got their first proper look at the impressive frontage of the famous stadium.

Rory's sulky mood evaporated in an instant. His vuvuzela was forgotten. The Doctor was right. This trip *was* a dream come true.

'Wow.' Rory came to a standstill. He stood and gawped, happily drinking in the scene. 'Wembley. Real, proper, old-style Wembley.' His face broke into a massive grin. 'Wicked!'

Chapter 3
The Man From FOOFA

The Empire Stadium at Wembley opened to the public in 1923. It hosted a wide range of sporting extravaganzas. Every season's FA Cup Final took place on the Wembley pitch, the World Speedway Championships were decided there, and in 1948 the stadium was the main venue for the London Olympic Games.

Rory, looking up at the famous Twin Towers, knew that the impressive list of Wembley events would run on into the stadium's future too: in thirty years' time, the final of Euro '96 would be decided there, and perhaps the most famous rock concert in history, Live Aid, would take place there in 1985, just before Rory was born. Right now, on 30 July 1966, Wembley was staging the event that would secure its place in football folklore forever; even though the grand old stadium would be demolished in 2003 to make way for a bigger, bolder Wembley, thanks to this day it would never be forgotten.

The forecourt was bustling with excited fans and full of the cries of opportunistic salespeople. Rory noticed a stand selling England rosettes, along with ones in the colours of the top teams of the elite First Division.

Another yelling vendor moved through the crowd not far off. 'Getcha match programmes 'ere! Only two 'n' six!'

'Two what and six what, though?' the Doctor mumbled to himself, frowning. 'Or are we supposed to add the two and six together? Eight pounds, perhaps?' He turned to Rory and Amy. 'Is that a lot for a programme? Or not enough?' He dug around in his trouser pocket and pulled out a handful of coins, displaying them on the flat of his palm. 'We should be able to pay for one out of that little lot, don't you think?' He peered at the assortment of bronze, copper, silver and gold coins. 'Oooh – hang on!' he said, plucking a thin blue-tinged disc from the pile. 'That's a two hundred thousand Drooble Piece. Only worth anything if you're on Tartac Beta. Barely get you a cup of tea there.' He thrust the remaining coins at Rory. 'Two and six, the man said. If I were you, I'd try two of one sort and six of another. The little twelve-sided ones are rather nice.'

Rory took the money with a wry look. 'Thanks. That's a big help,' he said, and hurried away to accost the programme seller.

It wasn't long before he rejoined them, proudly waving a light blue match programme. 'Remind me to take this home with us,' he told Amy. 'They sell for a *fortune* on eBay.'

'I reckon our tickets would fetch a fair bit, too,' she agreed.

'Ah. Tickets. Yes.' The Doctor frowned again. 'Now, how much do you think they'll cost? A lot of bobs?'

Rory looked aghast. 'We don't have tickets? But there'll be none left! Not for a game like this!'

'Good point,' said the Doctor calmly. 'Simpler to do without, anyway.'

'But they'll not let us through the barriers!' said Rory.

The Doctor looked over at the main spectator entrance, through which the fans were steadily flowing.

'Then we'll not go in through the barriers.' He quickly cast his gaze across the rest of the stadium building. 'We'll go in . . . there!' He pointed to a small grey door in the stadium wall, some distance from the main ticket barriers. A uniformed security guard stood beside it.

'You sure?' said Rory. 'What about the guard? He's hardly going to let us just stroll past. I reckon that entrance is for staff only or something. Doesn't look like we're supposed to use it.'

'Which is exactly why we're going to,' said the Doctor brightly. 'All the best doors are meant for other people. As for getting past the guard – you forget, Rory, we have something *much* better than tickets.' He thrust his hand into the inside pocket of his jacket, then withdrew it, holding up a small, blank notepad.

'One access-all-areas stadium pass . . .'

The security guard took a good long look, first at the Doctor, then at his psychic paper. Then he looked back at the Doctor again.

'You'll have to excuse me, Mr –' the guard glanced back at the paper – 'Lineker. I'm afraid I've not heard of this Fair Organisation of Football Agency before. What exactly is it you do, sir?'

'Not heard of FOOFA?' The Doctor looked surprised. 'Why, my good man, we're one of the most important regulatory bodies in international sport! As the name suggests, it's our job to make sure that all major soccer competitions are organised in a fair, unbiased way.' He gestured to Rory, beside him. 'Herr Wilhelm here is from the West German Football Association. I have invited him to visit the team changing rooms to approve the facilities provided for the German squad. To assure him that there is no evidence of favouritism – cheap, shiny toilet tissue in one team's changing rooms, luxury four-ply in the other, that sort of thing.'

The guard raised his eyebrows.

'And the young lady?' he asked.

'I'm an interpreter,' Amy told the guard curtly. 'Herr Wilhelm doesn't speak any English.'

The guard checked the Doctor's credentials again.

'Very well, sir,' he said, with a nod. 'Your pass-card clearly states that you are authorised to visit all areas of the stadium.' He turned to Amy. 'Please tell the foreign gentleman that I trust he'll find everything above board. We English are very proud of our reputation for fair play.'

Amy turned to Rory. '*Eins zwei drei vier fünf!*' she barked at him, in her best German accent. '*Sechs sieben acht neun zehn!*'

Rory nodded first to her, then to the security guard, as though acknowledging his good wishes.

The guard unlocked the grey door, held it open for the 'FOOFA' visitors to pass through, then closed it behind them.

They found themselves in a narrow corridor. Its walls were hung with black-and-white photographs of famous Wembley winners.

The Doctor nudged Amy with one patched elbow, grinning. 'Good job our guard friend didn't know any German himself, eh, Pond?' he whispered. 'He might have wondered why you were reciting the numbers one to ten!'

'It's the only German I can remember!' Amy hissed back. 'I only did one term of it at school.'

Rory was already engrossed in looking at the old team photographs, but the Doctor bundled him along the corridor. 'Come on! Let's take a look around! We still have a little while before the match is due to start – plenty of time to find a good spot in the stands. I bet you'd like a peek at some of the bits that are usually off limits first, eh, Rory?'

The Doctor strode ahead to where the corridor met another, and turned left. Rory and Amy hurried along behind him. They hadn't gone far when the passageway's right wall became glass. There was a door labelled PRESS ROOM 1. The Doctor stopped and peered through the transparent partition. He turned and smiled at Rory. 'There you go, young man – how about that for starters!'

Rory and Amy, intrigued, peered through the window. The press room appeared to have been commandeered for other purposes. Its furniture had been completely rearranged. Chairs were stacked neatly against the walls. In the centre of the cleared floor was a square table. The only people in the room were four uniformed police officers. They were stationed at each of the table's corners, looking outwards. At the centre of the table stood a glass case. Something golden sparkled within it.

'Wow!' hissed Rory. 'That's the cup! The *actual* World Cup!'

'Are you sure?' said Amy. 'It doesn't look much like the pictures I've seen. I thought it was a globe? Like a little world, with a bunch of guys holding it up?'

'You're thinking of the current trophy,' said Rory. 'This one's the original. The Jules Rimet Trophy. It was replaced in 1970 with the one you're talking about, after Brazil won it for the third time and got to keep it.'

Amy looked at him and shook her head. 'Sometimes it frightens me how much of your brain is occupied with footy facts, Williams. You'll never get a girlfriend, you know.'

Rory grinned. 'It's named after the French FIFA president who had the idea for the World Cup in the first place,' he went on – he was enjoying having the chance to show off his knowledge. 'It's made out of solid gold, on a lapis lazuli base. It's meant to be Nike, the Greek goddess of victory. You can see her wings – look.'

Amy looked back at the trophy – and at the four burly police officers standing guard over it. 'They're not taking any chances with it, are they?' she said.

'You can't blame them,' said Rory. 'It's been stolen once already, just a few months back. They put it on display at this fancy stamp exhibition and someone walked off with it. They never found the thief, but the trophy turned up again a week later. A dog called Pickles sniffed it out, in the bottom of a hedge, when he was out for his morning walk.'

'Clever pooch!' said Amy.

'It gets stolen again later on, too. In 1983, from a bulletproof glass display cabinet in Brazil. That time, they never got it back.'

One of the police guards was now looking directly at them. His expression suggested that he found three faces pressed up against the window rather suspicious.

'Shall we move along?' suggested the Doctor.

They hastily drew away from the press room

window and set off along the corridor once more.
They passed several other side rooms, but the Doctor
strolled purposefully ahead.

'I for one want to see the players' area,' he told
them. 'That's right over at the east end.'

As they passed another door, Rory came to a halt.
There was a sign on it saying GENTLEMEN. A smaller
one underneath read OFFICIALS ONLY.

'Er, guys,' said Rory a little awkwardly. 'If the
match is going to last two hours, I could do with
popping in here beforehand.'

'Go on then,' said Amy. 'We'll wait.'

'I might be a couple of minutes,' said Rory. 'It's a
Gary Neville.'

Amy gave him a blank look.

'Number two,' Rory explained with a smirk, before
ducking through the changing-room door.

'Ew!' Amy grimaced. 'Like I needed to know that!'

The Doctor raised his eyebrows. 'Do you think
there's anything he can't put a soccer spin on?'

A few seconds later, they were both surprised to see
Rory reappear.

'That was quick!' said Amy.

Rory didn't reply for a moment. His cheery
expression had vanished. He looked like he had just
had a nasty shock.

'There's something in the toilet,' he told them gravely.

Amy pulled another face. 'Again, *way* more information than we need, Rory!'

'No, not like that!' said Rory. 'In one of the cubicles.' He looked from Amy to the Doctor, stony-faced. 'It's a body.'

Chapter 4

Dead Lucky

Inside, the changing room was much like any other. There was a slatted wooden bench running along one wall with clothes hooks mounted above it, a large sink with a mirror over it, a row of ceramic urinals and two toilet cubicles. But there was one unusual detail: in the gap beneath the closed door of the left-hand cubicle, the soles of a pair of shoes were just visible.

'It's a bloke,' said Rory in a half whisper. 'You can tell from his footwear.'

'Genius, Sherlock!' Amy said. 'Although, the fact that he's in the gents is a bit of a clue too, don't you think?'

The Doctor immediately strode to the closed cubicle and knocked on its door. 'Hello! Can you hear me? This is the Doctor!'

There was no answer.

'I already tried that,' Rory said. 'I even reached under and waggled one of his feet a bit. Nothing.'

'Do you think he's dead?' asked Amy.

'Hard to say without a closer look,' replied the Doctor. 'Could just be deeply unconscious. We need to get this door open.'

Amy expected him to produce his sonic screwdriver, but the Doctor just stared at the cubicle door.

'A bog-door lock shouldn't give your sonic much trouble, should it?' suggested Amy after a few moments.

The Doctor shook his head. 'The lock isn't the problem, Pond. The door opens inwards. Whoever's in there is squashed up against the other side. If they are alive, they won't thank us for squeezing them half to death trying to get the door open.'

'So we need to force it outwards somehow?' said Rory.

'Exactly. Which means using something as a lever . . . A-ha!' The Doctor pulled his rolled-up newspaper from his jacket pocket. With his other hand, he took out his sonic screwdriver, and, after a little twiddling of the controls, he touched its glowing tip to the end of the newspaper.

'If I can realign the carbon molecules into a lattice,' he muttered, 'it should increase the rigidity to a high enough degree.' He deactivated the sonic screwdriver and, without warning, gave the toilet door a firm whack with one end of the rolled-up newspaper. It made a loud metallic clang.

'Excellent! Total petrification. Good as an iron bar,' said the Doctor. He quickly set to work on the cubicle door, using the now-rigid newspaper like a crowbar. It didn't take him long to prise the door off its hinges. He and Rory lifted it clear.

The man inside the cubicle was lying on his left side with his head against the toilet pedestal. He was curled up, his knees drawn into his chest and his face covered by his raised forearms. He was dressed like many of the male supporters they had seen so far – in a smart suit, with a white shirt and tie.

Amy helped the Doctor to carefully drag the stranger out on to the changing-room floor, where there was room to examine him. As Rory checked for signs of breathing or a pulse, the Doctor scanned his sonic across the man's body. His expression remained grave.

'He is dead, right?' said Amy.

Rory nodded grimly. ''Fraid so.'

'Has been for about an hour,' confirmed the Doctor.

'He's not very old, is he?' said Amy sadly. The man looked to be in his mid-twenties. 'What happened, do you think?'

31

The Doctor was now carrying out a more thorough scan of the man's chest. 'Sudden death in humans is quite often due to a myocardial infarction –'

Amy frowned. 'My-old-cardy'll what?'

'A heart attack,' clarified Rory.

'Oooh! Get you,' cooed Amy, impressed.

'What?' said Rory. 'I am a nurse, Amy!'

'But there's no indication of heart failure in this chap's case,' continued the Doctor. 'In fact, he's a picture of health, inside and out. Other than being dead.'

'You think he died from something other than natural causes?' said Amy.

'Possibly. But there's no evidence of violence,' replied the Doctor. 'No swelling from a blow or bleeding from a wound. No trace of toxins, either.'

'Perhaps he had some sort of medical condition,' suggested Rory. He pulled back the man's right jacket sleeve to look at his wrist. 'Did they have medic-alert bracelets in the sixties?'

'Dunno,' said Amy. 'You could check his pockets.'

Rory quickly frisked the dead man. He slipped a wallet from an inside jacket pocket and tossed it to Amy. 'See what you can find out from that.'

Amy began eagerly rifling through the wallet's contents. There was a twinkle in her eye. 'This is just like one of those American cop dramas on TV, isn't it?' she said, with a clear note of excitement. 'An unknown corpse. You two, the guys who do all that forensic-y pathology stuff. Me, the glamorous, super-brainy detective trying to piece together the victim's identity.' Her face lit up. 'I'm in *CSI*! *CSI Wembley!*'

Both Rory and the Doctor glanced up from examining the body. Their disapproving looks wiped the smile off Amy's face. She adopted an expression of exaggerated seriousness. 'Sorry. Obviously I'm not *enjoying* this. Not when someone has died. That would be wrong. Clearly.'

'Found anything yet to suggest which "someone", Detective Inspector Pond?' the Doctor asked.

Amy turned her attention back to the wallet's contents. 'Not really,' she said. 'There's not much here. Nothing with an ID, anyway. No credit cards. But I guess people didn't carry plastic back in 1966, did they? There's just a couple of big old one-pound notes. Cute.'

She tried another compartment in the back of the wallet. 'Hang on. There's this, too.' She pulled out a small slip of paper, and took a closer look at it. 'It's some sort of receipt, I think. Dated yesterday. From William Hill. That's one of those betting shops, isn't it?'

'Let's have a look,' said Rory. Amy passed him the slip of paper.

'Yeah, it's a betting chit,' said Rory. 'He must have put some money on a horse. Someone's written on the back of it. "Hot to Trot. Two hundred to one. Ten pounds to win." '

Amy frowned. 'Hot to Trot?' she repeated. 'I've heard that somewhere before. I'm *sure* I have . . .' She clicked her fingers. 'Got it! It was when we stopped at that newspaper stand on the way here. There was a sports bulletin playing on that guy's radio. The lead story was about this no-hoper horse that had won a big race. Hot to Trot – that was definitely what it was called.'

Rory passed the betting chit back to her. 'Well, if you're right, this chap just won a small fortune. At those odds, he'd have picked up two grand in winnings. And, round about now, two thousand pounds is a *lot* of money. We're talking enough to buy a house.'

Amy looked at the dead man pityingly. 'What a rubbish time to snuff it. Like winning the lottery, then keeling over before you can spend it.'

'Do you think maybe he works here?' asked Rory.

'What makes you say that?' asked Amy.

'Well, how come he's allowed in here? "Officials only" it said on the door.'

Rory pulled something from the man's trouser

pocket. It was a piece of printed card, about ten centimetres square, in a leather sleeve. Rory looked it over.

'I think I just found my answer. Listen to this.' He read out the text from the card. '"VIP World Cup Final Stadium Pass. Issued to the winner of the Daily Express World Cup Spot-the-Ball Challenge."'

'Blimey,' said Amy. 'So this guy had just won a fortune on the horses *and* a nationwide newspaper competition. He was having a seriously lucky day, wasn't he?'

'Up until the moment of his sudden, lonely death, you mean?' said Rory.

'Point taken.'

The Doctor finished examining the body. He stood up, frowning. 'I can't find any obvious cause of death. Maybe there's a clue in *where* we found him . . .' He moved into the now-doorless cubicle, and began looking around inside. 'Why would he have locked himself in here, do you think?'

Rory gave the Doctor an amused look. 'Er, you mean apart from the obvious reason?'

'Yes, Rory, I do.' The Doctor lifted one side of the toilet cistern's cover. He buzzed his sonic over the water inside for a second or two. He replaced the cover, then lifted the lid of the toilet itself and peered into the bowl. 'There's no evidence of him having used the loo.'

Amy smirked at Rory. 'Not like when you've been, then.'

Rory ignored her. 'How can you tell?' he asked the Doctor. 'He'd have flushed it, wouldn't he?'

'The water in the cistern is at room temperature,' explained the Doctor. 'Which means it's been in there long enough to equalise with its surroundings. This toilet hasn't been flushed for several hours.'

'I'm losing that cool cop-show vibe now,' muttered Amy. 'They tend not to major in loo flushing . . .'

'Maybe he was just about to go,' said Rory.

Amy looked despairing. 'Enough already with the detailed toilet analysis! Can't we dust for DNA or something?'

'Or maybe,' the Doctor pressed on, ignoring her, 'he wasn't in there to use the toilet at all. Look at how he's lying. Back curved, knees up, hands covering his face. The foetal position. The posture of an unborn child. Humans instinctively revert to it when they feel defenceless. And look at his eyes. They're screwed tight shut.'

Amy looked at the Doctor. 'You're saying he came here, locked himself in and curled up in a ball because he was frightened?'

'Exactly, Pond.'

'Frightened of what?' said Rory.

'No idea,' said the Doctor. 'But I intend to find out.' He knelt beside the man's body again. 'I must have missed something . . . I'll take another set of bio-readings. You two check if he has anything else on him.'

Rory obediently began a repeat search of the man's trouser pockets. Amy rooted around in his jacket to see if Rory had overlooked anything there.

After a few seconds of silence, the Doctor let out a triumphant cry. 'Ah-hah! Now *that* makes things a lot more interesting!' He was running the tip of his sonic slowly across the man's forehead.

'What is it, Doctor?' asked Amy.

'I can't find any evidence of endorphins anywhere in his system. Not even the faintest of traces. There shou–'

But, before the Doctor could explain further, something happened that brought their investigation to an abrupt halt: the changing-room door swung open and a tall middle-aged man strode through. He was smartly dressed and carrying a large green kitbag. He had silver hair, very dark, thick eyebrows and an impressive, almost black moustache.

The man stopped dead in his tracks, his shock

obvious in his face. Amy, Rory and the Doctor could hardly have looked more suspicious. A group of strangers, in a restricted area, going through the pockets of a corpse.

The man's wide-eyed gaze flitted to the forced cubicle door propped against the wall behind them, then back to the trio.

Amy smiled sweetly. This was going to take a *lot* of explaining.

Chapter 5
The Russian Linesman

The man with the moustache let his kitbag drop to the floor. He stepped towards the three friends, scowling fiercely, and growled something accusingly at them in a language that neither Rory nor Amy understood.

The Doctor was on his feet in a flash. He hurried to greet the newcomer.

'Hello there!' he said, beaming amiably. 'The name's Lineker! We're here from FOOFA. Having a spot of bother, as you can see!'

The man growled something else incomprehensible. It sounded equally hostile.

'Yes, I can imagine this must look *very* bad from where you're standing,' said the Doctor, still smiling.

'What dark thoughts must be running through that mind of yours, eh?'

As he said this, he gave the scowling stranger a harmless tap on the forehead with his rolled newspaper, which was still clutched in his left hand – at least, it was meant to be harmless.

What the Doctor had forgotten, for an absent-minded moment, was that the paper was now as hard as iron. The blow sent the moustached man staggering backwards. His heels hit his discarded kitbag and he toppled helplessly over it. As he fell, the back of his head hit one corner of the tiled wall. He slumped to the floor and lay still.

'Oh, great!' cried Amy. She and Rory jumped up and came to join the mortified Doctor. He was already bent over his unintended victim, hastily checking his vital signs.

'Nice going, Doctor!' said Amy. 'Nothing keeps a murder mystery alive like another dead body. Forget *CSI* – this is getting more like an Agatha Christie plot. Or Cluedo. "It was the Doctor, in the changing room, with the iron newspaper."'

'I haven't *killed* him, Amy!' said the Doctor defensively. 'He's just unconscious.' He continued to administer first aid, the sonic screwdriver buzzing.

Rory, meanwhile, was staring at the newcomer's

face. 'That's weird,' he muttered. 'I've seen this
bloke before. I'm certain I have. I recognise that
tash . . .'

He bent down to unzip the stranger's kitbag, and
began rummaging inside. The first thing he pulled out
was a small orange flag on a short wooden stem. This
he replaced, then lifted out an item of clothing. It was
a black long-sleeved sports shirt with white cuffs and
collars. Rory examined the name label stitched inside
the collar.

The colour drained rapidly from Rory's face. 'Oh,
no,' he mumbled. 'No, no, no . . .'

'What's the matter?' Amy looked at the black shirt
Rory was staring at with such obvious dismay. 'That's
a referee's kit, isn't it?'

'Not a referee's,' replied Rory miserably. 'This
bloke is a match official, all right, but not the ref – he's
a linesman. Tofiq Bahramov. The Russian linesman.'

'Azerbaijani,' said the Doctor, without looking up.

'Bless you,' said Amy.

'No. This man – he's from Azerbaijan, not Russia,'
explained the Doctor. 'In Eastern Europe. It's obvious
from his accent.'

'Yeah, right. Obvious,' said Amy. 'If you're some
sort of anorak-y accent spotter.'

'The term is "linguist", Pond.'

'Okay, okay,' said Rory impatiently. 'So maybe he's from Azerbaijan, not Russia. Whatever. All I know is he's famous as the "Russian Linesman".'

'Famous?' Amy looked at Rory. 'Famous how?'

'I can't believe you don't know! I thought everyone English knew about th–'

Rory noticed the fiery glint behind Amy's narrowing eyes just in time. Amy was Scottish, not English, and it didn't pay to forget it.

'He's famous for helping England beat Germany in the sixty-six final,' Rory stated simply.

'What – you mean he cheated? The match was fixed?'

'No, nothing as dodgy as that. He made a really tough call in England's favour. The whole match was finely balanced – two goals apiece after ninety minutes. Then Hurst scored another in extra time to put England three–two up, only it wasn't a *definite* goal. Hurst's shot hit the crossbar and rebounded down on to the goal line. It only counted because the Russian linesman – Bahramov here – told the referee that the ball had crossed the line.'

'Shame they didn't have goal-line technology,' observed Amy.

Rory stared at her. He was clearly stunned to hear her offer such an informed opinion.

'What?' said Amy. 'I read about it somewhere. About some dodgy decision in the 2010 World Cup. When Frank Lampard scored, but the ref said the ball hadn't crossed the line. And about how it wouldn't have happened if they'd had goal-line technology – whatever that is.'

Rory stuffed the linesman's shirt back into the kitbag.

'It still makes me sick just thinking about that Lampard no-goal,' he said bitterly. 'That was against Germany too. It would have made it two–two. Instead we lost four–one.' He shook his head sadly. 'A lot of England fans think that decision sealed the match.'

Rory pointed at the unconscious linesman – the Doctor was still bent over him, busy with his sonic screwdriver. 'This bloke made a crucial decision just like that back in sixty-six. Only then, it was in the final and it went England's way. He plays a vital part in England's victory – and the Doctor has just knocked his lights out!'

At that moment the Doctor stood up, looking greatly relieved.

'There, all done!' He noticed Rory's glum expression. 'Don't worry, Rory! He'll make a full recovery. I've triggered the blood vessels around the point of impact to dilate, so there's no danger of compression. And I've made sure he'll stay under for a little while. Won't wake for at least a couple of hours, I shouldn't think. That'll give the accelerated tissue repair I've set in motion more than enough time to take effect. When he comes round, he'll be right as rain.'

If anything, Rory looked even more miserable. 'You're totally missing the point, Doctor! Didn't you hear what I've been saying? England needs Bahramov at the match! He's going to miss it now, isn't he? When he doesn't turn up, he'll be replaced by someone else – someone who might not allow England's third goal. Which means the result could go a different way. We might not win.' He glared at the Doctor accusingly. 'There's a good chance you've just single-handedly lost us the World Cup!'

Chapter 6
A Changed Man

Rory looked very disappointed that his dramatic announcement hadn't caused more of a stir. He clearly felt he had just dropped a bombshell; the Doctor and Amy were supposed to be horror-stricken. As it was, neither of them looked very bothered.

'Don't get your knickers in a twist, Rory,' said Amy. 'England'll probably still be okay. Even without this Bah-whatsit bloke. They're supposed to win four–two, aren't they? So they can spare one goal.'

'No!' protested Rory. 'That's not how football works! A big decision can tip a match one way or the other. If their third goal isn't allowed, the lads might lose heart. They'd be going into the last period of extra time all square. The result could go either way!'

'A replacement linesman might still award the goal, Rory,' pointed out the Doctor.

45

'He might, yeah!' Rory turned to Amy. 'And England could *probably* still win. But that's not good enough, is it? We're talking about the only time we've ever won the World Cup! And we may have messed that up!'

The Doctor still showed no sign of sharing Rory's panic, but his expression did become graver. He strode over to stand beside the body from the toilet cubicle. 'For the moment, Rory, I'm more worried about what happened to this lucky chap.'

'You mean *un*lucky,' Amy corrected him.

The Doctor shook his head. 'No, Pond. It's his recent good luck that interests me – I have an idea that it may hold the key to his death. And, if I'm right, there are more important things at stake than the World Cup.'

Amy frowned. 'What do you m–'

'More important than England winning the World Cup?' spluttered Rory. He was looking at the Doctor as if he had completely lost the plot. 'Like *what*?'

But if the Doctor had been about to explain his theory, he must have thought better of it.

'Never mind. You're probably right, Rory. We ought to do something about this Bahramov chap. If he's missing from the match, it is possible it could turn out differently. And the sixty-six World Cup Final isn't a piece of history I particularly want the responsibility for rewriting – even accidentally.'

He stared at Bahramov's unconscious body in silence for a few seconds, lost in thought. Then he clicked his fingers and returned to his usual animated self. 'Okay, Rory. Panic not. I have a plan. Right here –' he delved into the left-hand pocket of his tweed jacket, rooted about for a few moments, then pulled a face. 'Or perhaps here –' he tried the other pocket, and with a look of relief pulled out something small, metallic and disc-shaped, with a slim strap attached. 'Voila! The solution to our dilemma!'

'A watch?' said Rory. 'I've already got a watch. How is a watch going to help?'

'Not a watch. A shimmer,' announced the Doctor. 'A piece of highly advanced morphing technology manufactured by the master craftsmen of the Vinvocci. You know the Vinvocci? Green-skinned humanoids. Rather a lot of alarmingly spiky bits. Otherwise delightful. It's a stroke of luck I still have this on me. It's been in my pocket since our visit to the Neutrino Casino. Back on Vegas IV, remember?'

'You bet I do!' said Amy. 'I won't forget that poker game in a hurry. Who'd have guessed aliens played such a mean game of cards? Only time I've played against someone with *three* poker faces.

I was cleaning up, too, till that big, hairy goon ate my betting chips.'

'I did warn you, Pond. Never play cards with a Moslovian. Anyway, where was I? Ah, yes – Vegas. Do you recall the karaoke competition they were running in the casino bar?'

'Sure,' said Amy. 'All those awful Elvis Presley impersonators competing to be the Cosmic King. It's hard to forget. It was like *The X Factor* with aliens. Extra-terrestrial Factor.' She snorted. 'Although there was one of them who was pretty good. Came third, I think.'

The Doctor looked at her, raised his eyebrows, and gave an impish grin.

'No?!' Amy's brown eyes widened with surprise. 'You? Honest?'

'Uh-huh-huh!' replied the Doctor, Elvis-style.

'I wondered where you'd slunk off to!' said Amy, grinning. 'But that third-place guy didn't look anything *like* you! He was a dead ringer for Presley!'

'I was indeed,' agreed the Doctor. 'And all thanks to this little beauty.' He held up the shimmer. 'As I said, it's a morphing device. Changes what you look like – from the neck up, at least. It masks the wearer's physical appearance and projects a remarkably convincing fake one in its place.'

He took hold of Rory's left arm and began hastily fastening the shimmer round it, just above his normal wristwatch.

'A word of advice though, Rory –' the Doctor snapped closed the shimmer's magna-strap – 'leave it switched off until you need it. The masking field can make you feel quite ill once it's running. That's why I had to drop out of the last karaoke round in Vegas. Too queasy to make it through "All Shook Up".' He grinned. 'Ironic, really.'

Rory lifted his wrist and looked at the alien device now strapped to it, then back at the Doctor. He shook his head. 'No. Sorry. I'm not getting it. How will me looking like Elvis help? How does that change the fact you just took out the Russian linesman?'

'Azerbaijani,' said Amy. Rory scowled at her.

'You're not going to look like Elvis,' explained the Doctor impatiently. He quickly took out his sonic screwdriver and crouched down beside the unconscious Bahramov. He began slowly scanning the sonic's glowing tip back and forth across the linesman's face. 'A Vinvoccian shimmer can be programmed to mimic almost any physical appearance.'

He completed his forehead-to-chin scan of Bahramov's features and stood up. He turned back to Rory and took hold of his left wrist again, then gingerly touched the tip of his sonic to the flat face of the shimmer. He held it there for a few moments. There was a soft *bleep* from the shimmer and a pulse of red light swirled once round its outer rim.

'There!' said the Doctor. 'You're all set! I've overwritten the facial-modelling data. Give it a try. Just twist the dial casing to activate it.'

Rory still looked completely lost, but he did as he was told.

Amy's eyes widened with astonishment. 'Wow. Now that is properly spooky,' she said, impressed. She looked from Rory to the unconscious linesman, then back again. 'They're like twins! Even the tash is spot on.'

The Doctor smiled. He clapped Rory on the shoulder.

'So, problem solved!' he said cheerfully. 'One instant replacement Mr Bahramov. As long as you're wearing the shimmer and have it turned on, nobody will know you're not the real thing.'

Rory was slowly catching on. He pointed to the unconscious linesman. 'You want me to impersonate him?'

'It's not what *I* want, Rory. It's what *you* want,' replied the Doctor. 'To save the match, remember? "England expects" and all that. And don't look so worried. You'll do splendidly!'

He grabbed the real Bahramov's kitbag from the floor and thrust it at Rory. 'All you have to do is get changed into this little lot, and be out on the pitch in time for kick-off.'

'But –'

'Then you can personally see to it that the goal-line decision goes England's way, yes?'

'But I'm not –'

'Because you'll be the one making it. Simple. Can't fail. Well, not unless it does.'

Rory gave up. He silently took the kitbag from the Doctor, turned and skulked across to the changing bench, shaking his head the whole time.

'As for you and me, Pond –' the Doctor held his sonic screwdriver out at arm's length. He began moving it in arcs and sweeps, like an instrument of magic. He squinted intently at its luminous green tip for a few seconds. 'I think we should get ourselves over to the South Stand,' he muttered at last, fully focused on the sonic's flickers and pulses.

'You're still planning to watch the match, then?' asked Amy.

The Doctor appeared not to hear her. 'Actually, make that *under* the South Stand,' he added. He finally lowered the sonic screwdriver and turned to face Amy. 'We may have a little business to conduct there.'

'What kind of business?'

'But we probably ought to tidy up a bit first,' rambled the Doctor, failing once again to answer Amy. 'I should be able to patch up that door . . .' He looked at the pair of bodies lying on the floor. 'Let's get these two somewhere out of sight to start with. You grab our linesman friend –'

'*Doctor!*' Amy was getting annoyed. 'What kind of business?'

The Doctor gave her a cheery look. 'Oh, you know, Pond. Usual sort of thing.'

He reached down to grab the dead man's feet. As he began dragging the corpse towards the door, he looked over his shoulder at Amy. 'Just a deadly alien life form to hunt down.'

Amy watched the Doctor reverse out through the door. She gave a resigned sigh, bent down to grasp Bahramov's ankles and set off after him, dragging the unconscious linesman behind her.

'Course. Deadly alien hunt. Silly me for asking.'

Chapter 7

On the Spot

Rory was feeling extremely peculiar. The fact that he had now been wearing the shimmer for some time was undoubtedly one reason his insides felt like he was on a rough ferry crossing. The Doctor had warned him about this unfortunate side-effect of using the Vinvoccian device.

But it wasn't only the shimmer that was making Rory feel uncomfortable. The churning in his stomach was as much to do with the situation in which he now found himself. He was standing at the mouth of the Wembley players' tunnel, about to lead the teams out for the most momentous football match in English history, in front of a crowd of 93,000 screaming fans. Not to mention the largest-ever TV audience of over 32 million people. This wasn't the sort of thing that happened to most ordinary lads from Leadworth.

Rory glanced nervously at the two other match officials standing beside him. So far, neither of them seemed to have noticed anything suspicious. Apart from the side-effects, the shimmer was working a treat. Now that he was wearing Bahramov's full black-and-white kit, Rory was the spitting image of the Azerbaijani linesman. Even Bahramov's friends and family would not have seen through the disguise – unless they noticed that he had inexplicably lost a few centimetres in height.

Rory's biggest worry had been what to do if someone spoke to him. He might look like Bahramov, but he had no clever alien gadget to make him sound like the linesman. So far, however, he'd been lucky. He had only needed to return the occasional nod of acknowledgement, smile or gesture. In fact, it was becoming clear that none of the officials expected to talk much. Rory vaguely recalled something from a TV programme on the 1966 final about the language barrier between them. He was fairly sure the referee was from Switzerland. And the other linesman was Czech, wasn't he? If the three of them had no common language, he'd hopefully be able to bluff his way through whatever communication was required. The odd shout, hand signal or bit of flag-waving might just see him through . . .

Rory looked over his shoulder, back down the sloping concrete shaft of the players' tunnel, and felt his stomach do another cartwheel. The tunnel was crammed with footballing legends. At the head of the line of players on the right-hand side of the tunnel, wearing red shirts, white shorts and red socks, stood the blond-haired English captain, Bobby Moore. On the opposite side, the West German captain and centre-forward Uwe Seeler was in position to lead out his ten teammates. The Germans were wearing their white-and-black first kit.

Rory's eyes darted from player to player. There was Geoff Hurst; there Bobby Charlton, the legendary English midfielder, and his older brother Jackie; Alan Ball, the youngest in the squad, who would win Man of the Match in this epic final. And there, in the German line-up, a young Franz Beckenbauer, another of the greatest players of all time, who Rory knew would go on to captain the World Cup-winning team in 1974 *and* coach the German squad that triumphed in the 1990 tournament. These were footballers Rory had admired all his life. He had watched the black-and-white TV footage and glorious Technicolor Pathé films of their historic '66 clash many times. And now here they were, metres away, in the flesh.

A nudge from the referee drew Rory's attention.

The ref was tapping his stopwatch. It was evidently time for the teams to make their way out on to the pitch. Without further ado, the Swiss official led the way.

Rory took a deep breath, tried to get his insides to stop churning like a washing machine on spin, and set off after him.

A little over ten minutes later, Rory found himself one of a small group of five men – the three match officials and both team captains – gathered within the centre circle of the Wembley pitch.

The short spell since the teams had emerged from the players' tunnel had not been without a few sticky moments. During the teams' national anthems, Rory had been so caught up in the moment that he had very nearly joined in with the crowd's rousing rendition of 'God Save the Queen'. Thankfully, he had come to his senses just in time – a match official from Eastern Europe belting out the English anthem would have looked rather suspicious.

The Royal Box was directly above the stadium's main entrance tunnel. The world champions would climb the famous thirty-nine steps that ran up to it to receive their winners' medals from Her Majesty, Queen Elizabeth II. Rory had a good view of the dark-haired queen in her striking yellow coat and hat. He was struck by how young she looked.

After the anthems, the English and German teams had shaken hands, then jogged out across the pitch's 'hallowed turf' to warm up. The players began kicking about the match balls they had carried out with them, and Rory had noted how basic they were. The plain, orangey-brown leather balls looked a lot less flashy than the high-spec ones used in top-level football in the twenty-first century.

There were many other ways in which the scene around him differed greatly from the world of football with which he was familiar. For one thing, many of the spectators were standing – Rory was used to modern all-seater stadiums. For another, fans from both nations were mixed in together – West German flags waved here and there among a sea of Union Jacks.

There was no dugout for coaches and substitutes. In fact, there was no substitutes' bench full stop. Player substitutions hadn't been allowed in early tournaments, Rory had recalled. Only four men sat on the England team bench at the side of the pitch: the manager and his coaching team, all wearing pale blue tracksuits.

But, before Rory had had time to take in more than these few details, he found himself being led by the Swiss referee to the centre of the pitch. Now, as he stood at the very heart of it all, with kick-off only moments away, he continued to marvel at the noise and spectacle. The volume of the crowd had risen even further. The atmosphere was like nothing he had ever experienced.

He watched Moore and Seeler, the team captains, exchange national tokens and shake hands sportingly. Then they stepped back to allow the referee room for the coin toss. Rory, looking on, found it rather bizarre to be the only person in the ground who already knew that Moore would win the toss and choose to let the Germans take the kick.

As Moore withdrew from the centre circle, the referee turned to Rory and his fellow linesman, and gestured to his watch once more. He was signalling for them to check their timekeeping devices, Rory realised, so as to be sure they were synchronised.

Rory instinctively went to pull up his left sleeve in order to check his watch – then changed his mind. Exposing his shimmer would be a very bad idea. The advanced alien technology of the Vinvocci did not belong in the '60s. Besides, having *two* watches would seem weird enough. Instead, he slipped his hand under the cuff of his sleeve and glanced down, pretending to check.

A moment later, the referee gestured for both linesmen to take up their positions. The Czech official jogged off towards the touchline in front of the South Stand. Rory gratefully hurried away to take up his own assigned position. It would be his job – or rather Bahramov's – to keep an eye on play within the half of the pitch furthest from the players' tunnel. England would start the match defending his end.

As he crossed the pitch, Rory felt his pulse quickening. His experience as a football official was limited, to say the least: one stint as referee at an informal match after a friend's wedding, between the bride and groom's relatives. That was it. And that game had ended in a brawl. Here he was, at Wembley, trying to pass himself off as a linesman of international standing.

Anxious last-minute thoughts flooded Rory's brain. Even some of the laws of the game were different back in 1966, weren't they? Wasn't the goalkeeper only allowed three strides carrying the ball or something? And what about passing back to the keeper? The rules about that had changed, too, hadn't they?

Rory's mind was racing as he reached the touchline. Feeling sicker than ever, he turned to face the field of battle. The players had already taken up their positions. Somewhere beneath his panic and nausea, Rory registered the familiar formations: Germany were playing four up front, with wingers; England had a four-four-two shape, with Nobby Stiles in a slightly deeper, more defensive position than his three fellow midfielders.

The two German centre-forwards were at the spot now. Seeler had the ball at his feet. Rory saw the referee put his whistle to his lips, and heard its shrill blast. He gripped the wooden shaft of his linesman's flag more tightly.

They were off.

Chapter 8
The South Stand

Amy peered ahead into the gloom and frowned. She turned to the Doctor, who was fiddling with his sonic screwdriver beside her.

'So what exactly am I looking out for, Doctor? An itsy-bitsy cute-looking alien or something a bit more, you know –' she pulled a monster-style face, clawed at the air with her hands and stomped her feet.

'Embarrassing?' ventured the Doctor.

Amy scowled. 'I was doing "scary".'

She and the Doctor had now spent ten minutes or more searching the area under the South Stand. They had gained entry through a locked (but not for long) maintenance doorway. The Doctor had led the way into the murky forest of dark grey columns that lay beyond – the sturdy metal struts of the grandstand's steel skeleton. He had kept his eyes fixed on the

flickering tip of his sonic screwdriver. Amy had
followed, ducking under crossbeams now and again,
and trying not to stumble on the rough concrete
underfoot. With only the glow of the sonic to light
their way, it was fairly slow going. By now Amy
thought they *must* have been right under the centre of
the grandstand.

So far, there had been no sign of any alien creature.

'Sorry, Pond,' said the Doctor. 'Haven't a clue what
it looks like, I'm afraid. All we know is that it's some
kind of Luck-sucker.'

'Excuse me?'

'A Luck-sucker. A neural parasite.'

'Again, excuse me?'

The Doctor left off recalibrating his sonic
screwdriver for a moment to give Amy his full
attention. 'We know that poor chap back in the gents
had been on a remarkable run of good fortune prior to
his death. Yes?'

Amy nodded.

'After the run of luck he'd been having,' continued
the Doctor, 'he must have been feeling on top of the
world this morning. His blood would have contained
unusually high levels of endorphins.'

'Which are?' said Amy. 'In normal-person speak,
please.'

'Hormones which make you feel euphoric,' explained the Doctor. 'They generate the feel-good rush.'

'Yup, remembering now!' said Amy. 'Eating chocolate makes you release them, right?'

'Indeed – among other things. The point is, they're linked with the sort of emotional high our friend must have been on. But my bio-scans picked up no trace of any recent endorphin surge. Quite the opposite, in fact – from my sonic readings, you would have thought the poor fellow hadn't felt happy in days.'

'So the guy was a bit of a misery.' Amy gave a shrug. 'Why has that got us hunting aliens?'

'He wasn't a bit of a misery, Amy. He must have felt delighted – ecstatic, even – when he won that horse-racing bet. But something drained every trace of that positive energy from his body.'

'Our mystery alien?'

'Exactly,' said the Doctor. 'I've come across several species that feed on the positive neural energy of others. Neural parasites. They target those experiencing high levels of good fortune and extremes of happiness, and drain the resulting positive energy from them. Some folk call them Happiness Vampires, or Luck-suckers.'

Amy shivered. 'Sounds creepy. Kinda like the Dementors in *Harry Potter.*'

'I suppose,' replied the Doctor. 'Some species only drain off small quantities of neural energy, then move on. The host is left relatively unharmed – just a little low-spirited. But others drain everything they can –'

'And you end up dead in a toilet.'

'Not necessarily in a toilet. But dead, yes.'

'So that's what we're looking for?' said Amy. 'An alien Luck-sucker?'

The Doctor nodded.

'And you're sure it's under here somewhere?'

'Almost certain.' The Doctor held up his sonic screwdriver. Its tip was pulsing regularly. 'I'm picking up clear signs of non-human life-form activity. My sonic screwdriver detected them even back in the changing room.'

'Couldn't they be coming from rats or something?' suggested Amy. 'Or really big spiders?' She paused. 'On second thoughts, I might prefer a happiness-draining alien.'

'No, it's something non-terrestrial. Or I'm a Raxacoricofallapatorian.'

The Doctor slowly scanned the sonic screwdriver to his right. His face lit up as its tip flared brightly.

'There! You see!' The Doctor excitedly thrust the screwdriver towards Amy. 'Look at that, Pond! If it was all just concrete and steel under here, I wouldn't be getting a bio-thermal reading like that, now, would I?'

Amy hadn't the faintest idea which bit of the sonic screwdriver she was supposed to be looking at. 'Absolutely not,' she said solemnly. 'That would be silly.'

'Come on!' The Doctor turned to his right and strode away purposefully. 'This way!'

Amy did her best to keep up, picking her way through the maze of metal girders as fast as she could – but she spotted one crossbeam a moment too late.

'Ow!' She stopped to nurse her head. She had hit it quite hard. 'Arrrggh!' she growled. 'Whatever that wretched alien is, I wish it had picked a nicer place to hang out!'

The Doctor didn't reply. He had come to an abrupt halt just ahead of her. He had suddenly become very still, and was peering ahead into the gloom.

'Doctor?'

He turned, eyes sparkling. 'You've put your finger right on it again, Pond,' he whispered excitedly.

Amy looked defensive. 'What?' she hissed back, not sure why they were whispering. 'I didn't touch anything!'

'No, I mean, look!' The Doctor bundled her forward, and pointed into the gloom. 'A place to hang out is *exactly* what they were after . . .'

Up ahead, about twenty metres or so from where she and the Doctor were standing, Amy could make out pale shapes amid the darkness. As she concentrated her gaze, the Doctor increased the intensity of his sonic screwdriver's glow a little, to cast a bit more light.

Dangling from one of the higher crossbeams of the grandstand's metal framework was a row of twenty or so large, sac-like pale grey objects. Each of the flabby capsules was nearly three metres long, and had a slight ribbing to its shape, like the body of a maggot. The sacs hung from the girder by thick bands of sticky-looking webbing. They glistened, as though wet.

Midway along the row, Amy saw two sacs that looked different from the rest: they were ripped from top to bottom, as though they had burst. She could see that they were empty inside, except for the almost luminous silvery ooze that coated their inner walls.

Amy flinched – one of the sacs next to the burst ones had twitched, as though something inside it had moved.

'Look! There are more over there!' hissed the Doctor.

Amy followed his gaze. Away to the left, a second row of grey sacs dangled from another grandstand beam. She could just make out more rows in the murk behind them, too. There must have been hundreds.

Amy had no idea what was inside the peculiar grey sacs – or, in the case of the two burst ones, what *had* been inside them. But she knew one thing for sure: they gave her the creeps.

Big time.

Chapter 9
Not Quite Butterflies

'What are they, Doctor?' hissed Amy.

'Vispic leeches.' The Doctor smacked the heel of one palm against his tall forehead. 'Of course! Vispics fit our suspect profile perfectly.' He stared at the row upon row of dangling sacs. 'But I've never seen a brood so large –'

At that moment a pinpoint of orange light appeared in the darkness ahead of them.

'And it looks like they're still arriving,' murmured the Doctor.

The dot of light flared and widened, quickly becoming a perfect circle nearly a metre across. Amy had the distinct impression that the light was shining *through* the circle as though it was a hole in the air, admitting the orange glow from somewhere behind it.

She watched in horror as something pale and wet began to wriggle out of the hole in the air. A bulbous, maggoty body slowly squirmed its way through. It was off-white, with blotches of grey. Its flattened head – if that was what the first end to appear was – was dotted with dark, fibrous patches. It reminded Amy of the exposed surface of a verruca.

Dragging its tail end free, the wriggling thing flopped on to the concrete floor with an unpleasant squelch. The luminous hole it had come through immediately shrank back to the size of a pinpoint, then vanished.

Amy watched, transfixed, as the creature slowly squirmed itself across the floor to one of the vertical steel columns. It began to wriggle its way up towards a horizontal beam from which several of the pale grey sacs already dangled.

'Is that what's inside each of those pouchy things?' Amy asked the Doctor.

'The cocoons? Yes.'

'Yuck.' Amy watched the creature squirm slowly up the column. 'It doesn't look particularly deadly, though,' she observed. 'Gross, yeah. But not dangerous.'

The Doctor gave her a dark look. 'Tell that to our friend from the changing room.'

'But how did one of those things even get near him?' asked Amy. 'They look way too . . . sluggy to corner anyone.'

'They didn't need to corner him,' said the Doctor. 'Vispics can drain neural energy from a host without any physical contact. As long as they can get within a reasonable range, they can feed at will. From under here, they'd have been able to latch on to that poor chap we found without any difficulty. Once they'd begun feeding, he would have felt a growing sense of inexplicable unhappiness, fear and ultimately utter terror. It would have driven him to lock himself away, in a desperate attempt to hide – though he would have had no idea what from.'

'Sounds horrible,' said Amy.

'Indeed. And, as the Vispics drained away the last of his neural energy, he would simply have lost the will to live.' The Doctor shook his head sadly. 'Dreadful.'

He was silent for a moment or two.

'Don't be fooled into thinking that Vispics are always sluggish, Pond. You're looking at their young, their larval form. They're a species that metamorphose as they mature – they change form entirely. In time, given the right conditions, an adult leech will emerge from each of those cocoons.' The

71

Doctor peered across at the nearest row of dangling sacs. 'In fact, judging by those burst ones, I'd say some already have.'

Amy was still watching the larva in horrified fascination. It had now squirmed its way out along the horizontal girder, and was busy securing its tail end to it with a blob of sticky goo it had just secreted.

'So – they're sort of like caterpillars turning into butterflies?'

'A little bit, yes,' said the Doctor. 'If you can imagine a caterpillar that feeds on neural energy rather than cabbage. And, instead of a butterfly, a large, ultra-intelligent, ruthless predator. With pincers. And no pretty wings.'

'The grown-ups are that bad, huh?'

'If you're after classic chase-you-and-eat-you scary, Pond, an adult Vispic is about as good as it gets.'

Amy gave him a hard look. 'You say that like you're impressed. Got a real thing for monsters, haven't you? It's like being out and about with one of those loony wildlife presenters who only seek out the deadliest animals. The ones who like prodding snakes or winding up crocodiles . . .'

'The biology of the Vispics certainly fascinates me,' admitted the Doctor. 'Their adult form is really quite something.' His voice suddenly dropped to the quietest of whispers. 'But don't take my word for it. See for yourself!'

Three large, unearthly creatures had just become visible in the gloom up ahead. They each had a long, flattened body shape, which broadened suddenly at both head- and tail-end. Their hammer-headed, hammer-tailed bodies moved on six multi-jointed legs. Their fourth and foremost two limbs were hideously outsized and ended in cruel crescent-shaped claws.

The creatures' midsections still retained something of the bulbous, maggoty shape of their larval form but, instead of blotched white, their bodies were now darker and covered all over in a strange, shifting multicoloured sheen like a film of oil on water.

One of the creatures was significantly larger than the other two. *Older, perhaps*, thought Amy. They were moving about under the dangling cocoons, as though patrolling.

'Keep very still!' the Doctor mouthed at her. 'They don't know we're here – yet.'

'Great, I really am in a wildlife documentary,' Amy hissed back. 'How can you tell?'

'Because as soon as they do sense us, they'll attack. And there's a very obvious sign when that's about to happen.'

'Which is?'

To Amy's astonishment, the largest of the three adult Vispics suddenly disappeared. Completely.

'That!' cried the Doctor. '*Run!*'

Chapter 10
A Deadly Brood

Amy and the Doctor covered the distance to the maintenance doorway a lot faster than they had on their outwards trek. The adrenaline rush brought on by a large alien predator chasing her worked wonders for Amy's girder-dodging skills: as she sprinted after the Doctor, she ducked, sidestepped and hurdled obstacles like an athlete.

Not far behind her, she could hear the clatter of inhuman feet on concrete. There was the occasional ring of claw on metal – presumably the sound of the pursuing Vispic scrabbling over or squeezing through the steel supports of the grandstand's frame.

Amy glanced over her shoulder only once. Despite the noises, there was nothing to see. She turned back and kept running, her heart pounding.

Then, thank goodness, there was the door. The

Doctor narrowly beat her to it. He flung it open, bundled Amy through, then dived after her.

The light in the corridor was dazzling after the darkness under the stand. Screwing up her eyes against the glare, Amy helped the Doctor to pull the maintenance door closed. He urgently applied his sonic screwdriver to the door's lock to secure it.

An instant later, something heavy slammed into the other side of the door. Amy heard the sound of something sharp scrabbling and screeching against the opposite side for a few seconds. Then silence fell.

The Doctor, breathing heavily, leaned his back against the door and slid down into a sitting position. He brushed his unruly hair – which was wilder than ever after their mad dash – out of his eyes.

'Phew!' He gave Amy a broad grin. 'Invigorating stuff, eh, Pond? That's got my hearts pumping!'

Amy flopped down next to him. She was too busy trying to get her breath back to reply for a few moments.

'Do you think it's gone?' she said at last. She put her ear to the door. 'I can't hear anything.'

'I imagine it's returned to the cocoons,' said the Doctor. 'Its priority will be to protect them.'

'How did it just vanish like that?'

The Doctor gave her a smug look. 'I told you their

biology was mightily impressive, Pond. Adult Vispics have remarkably sophisticated camouflage. They can adjust the pigmentation of every area of their skin – change the colour of any part of their body at will.'

'Like a chameleon?'

'Sort of,' said the Doctor. 'But a Vispic's ability to match its appearance to its background is much more advanced. Its sensory organs can pinpoint the exact position of any other living thing in its proximity. The Vispic analyses the precise background against which that particular observer is viewing it, then matches its skin pattern to it exactly, making itself more or less impossible to see.'

Amy looked thoughtful. 'But if their camouflage works like that, they could only hide themselves from one person at a time, couldn't they?' she asked. 'I mean, if two or three people were hanging around near a Vispic, they'd each see it against a different background, right? Depending on where they were. It couldn't blend in with *all* those backgrounds.'

'Clever girl, Pond. Absolutely right. If there are multiple observers near it, the Vispic has to try to take their different perspectives into account. It calculates the ideal camouflage pattern for each, then alternates between them very, very quickly. Its camouflage becomes less effective. You'd be able to perceive its body as a flickering area in your vision. The more people the Vispic tries to conceal itself from, the more skin patterns it has to cycle through, and the more obvious the flicker.'

'So, if you've got plenty of company, you've a chance of keeping track of where it's got to? But if it only has to hide itself from you, it can pretty much disappear?'

'Precisely.'

'So they're big, hungry and invisible.' Amy raised her eyebrows. 'Lovely. Remind me to add them to my Top Ten Favourite Aliens list.'

'Their only flaw as a predator is their modest speed,' the Doctor told her. 'They're not particularly quick on their feet. But if your prey can't see you, then you don't have to be especially fast to make a kill.'

'But what are they doing at Wembley?' asked Amy.

'Vispics are parasites. They have only one motivation – to find hosts.'

'I meant, how did they get here?'

'In larval form, they have the ability to spatially displace themselves.'

Amy gave the Doctor a look. 'You're talking Time Lord again.'

'They can burrow through space,' the Doctor said. 'You saw one do it under the stand. That larva was cutting a dimensional wormhole to allow itself into Earth space. Spatial displacement.'

Amy remembered the glowing orange circle in mid-air.

'It's how they live,' the Doctor continued. 'First, locate a food source – a host population from which they can drain neural energy. Then pupate. Wrap up snug in a cocoon within feeding range of that population. From there, they soak up the energy they need to metamorphose. When they've fed enough to transform, they emerge as carnivorous adults. The adults prey on what remains of the host population. They lay eggs, which hatch into larvae, and the cycle starts again.'

'Charming. Not great pets, then.'

'It's no surprise that the Vispics have discovered Earth at this particular point in its history,' said the Doctor. 'The Space Race between the United States and the Soviet Union is flat out, driving technology forward. Rockets, probes, satellites – they're all taking off about now, literally. Earth has just arrived on the galactic scene. And has obviously attracted some unwelcome attention . . .'

'But why Wembley?' said Amy. 'It seems a pretty random place to choose.'

'The Vispic larvae are luck-suckers, remember.

They feed on euphoria and joy. Right now, this stadium is packed with tens of thousands of football fans, all eagerly anticipating that their nation is about to win the World Cup.' The Doctor swept back his drooping fringe with long fingers. 'To a Vispic, the supporters' excitement probably smells like bacon frying. They've sensed an oncoming feast. If England wins, the leech larvae will be within feeding range of thousands of deliriously happy fans. They'll gorge themselves. There'll be enough positive energy for every Vispic we saw cocooned under there to metamorphose into an adult.'

Amy didn't need the Doctor to tell her what would follow – what the horrific consequences of hundreds of hungry adult Vispics let loose on the streets of London would be. It didn't bear thinking about.

'So, what do we do, Doctor? How do we stop that happening?'

The Doctor raised his eyebrows. 'Not sure yet.' His expression changed to a frown. 'What puzzles me is how so many larvae have come to displace themselves to the same location. It suggests that they're being called, somehow. And if that is the case . . .'

His voice trailed off as his nine-hundred-and-something-year-old mind wrestled with this latest catastrophic problem.

Amy tried desperately to think of something.

'I see what you meant now,' she said, after a few moments. 'Back in the gents.'

'Hmm?'

'When you told Rory that there might be more important things than the World Cup at stake.'

The Doctor suddenly leapt to his feet and gave an excited whoop. 'That's it! Of course! The cup!' He looked down at the startled Amy, his eyes alight. 'Pond, we have to get our hands on that trophy! Come on!'

And, without further explanation, he sprinted away along the corridor.

Amy hauled herself to her feet, scowling. 'Not you as well,' she grumbled. 'It's bad enough having a soccer-obsessed husband. What is it with boys? It's only a stupid game . . .'

With a long-suffering sigh, she set off to catch up with the Doctor.

Chapter 11

Half-time

To Rory's great astonishment and relief, he had made it through the first half without being rumbled.

He had fully expected to make a howler of a touchline decision at some point, which would expose him as an impostor. He had also worried that forty-five minutes of the shimmer's sickening side-effects might prove too much for him. Thankfully, neither of these fears had come true.

In fact, he had been rather fortunate so far in the way the match had unfolded. There had been little need for either linesman to get involved. West Germany's early goal in the twelfth minute had been at Rory's end of the pitch. Helmut Haller had fired in his shot after England's usually rock-solid left-back Ray Wilson had failed to clear a German cross. But, as there was no suggestion of offside, the referee had

awarded the goal without having to consult Rory.
Hurst had equalised for England six minutes later, at
the other end of the pitch, which was the other
linesman's area of responsibility. Apart from a handful
of relatively straightforward throw-in decisions, when
Rory had only needed to flag whose throw it was, he
had had little to do.

The half-time score of 1–1 meant that so far, at
least, the match was still on track, despite the real
Bahramov's absence. But Rory knew he wasn't out of
the woods yet. Not by a long way. He still had to
survive another full hour of play – and nausea – before
he could make the all-important goal-line decision.
Only that would guarantee England's victory and
prevent history from unravelling.

Right now, though, he had a more immediate
challenge. He had to get through the half-time interval
without blowing his cover.

When the referee's whistle blast signalled the end
of the first forty-five minutes, Rory didn't hang
around. He made sure he was the first of the three
match officials to leave the pitch and swiftly headed for
their private changing rooms. Once there, he
immediately locked himself in a toilet cubicle and
deactivated his shimmer.

The relief was immediate and immense. For the

first time in nearly an hour, Rory didn't feel as though he was about to throw up.

He sat on the toilet with its lid down, enjoying a few minutes of normal-feeling insides, and hoping to stay well out of everyone's way until he could return to the touchline for the second half.

Ten minutes or so passed. Rory didn't hear anybody else enter the changing room. Perhaps the referee and Czech linesman wouldn't need to use it during the interval. That would suit him just fine.

Hiding in the cubicle was giving Rory the slight creeps. After all, it was in the cubicle next door that he had found the dead man just over an hour ago. Rory had purposely not shut himself in there. He wondered if the Doctor and Amy had made any progress figuring out what had happened to the poor man. He wondered, too, where they had decided to hide the real Bahramov till he awoke . . . and whether they had managed to catch any of the first half of the match.

His thoughts were interrupted by the clatter of studs on the concrete floor. The noise rose to a crescendo, then began to fade. The players had passed the changing room, heading back to the tunnel for the second half.

When he was confident that the last player had

gone by, Rory emerged from the toilet cubicle
and slipped out into the corridor, planning to follow
the players back out on to the pitch at a discreet
distance.

'What are you doing down here, young man?'

Rory spun round guiltily. He found himself face-
to-face with a middle-aged gentleman in a pale blue
tracksuit with red, white and blue cuffs. Rory
recognised the man's stern face instantly; he had seen
many photographs of it in football memorabilia and
magazines. It belonged to Alf Ramsey, the England
team manager.

Heart pounding, Rory groped hopelessly for a
reply.

'You're not one of the match officials,' growled
Ramsey, before Rory could think of what to say.
'What business have you got in their changing rooms?'

An alarm sounded somewhere in Rory's brain.
Why didn't Ramsey recognise him as Bahramov the
linesman?

His heart sank.

He had forgotten to turn the shimmer back on.

'Ah! I . . . er . . .' stammered Rory, now completely
flustered. 'I'm one of the reserve officials!'

'Reserve officials?' This role was clearly new to the
English boss.

'Uh-huh, yeah,' Rory blundered on. 'Er . . . you know . . . in case any of the original three need substituting,' he suggested hopefully.

Ramsey continued to glare at him suspiciously.

'New FOOFA rules,' Rory explained. 'To ensure fair play.'

Ramsey's frown deepened. 'FOOFA?'

'That's right!' Rory was floundering. 'Anyway . . . enough about me!' He tried desperately to change the subject. 'How do *you* feel the game is going so far, Mr Ramsey?' He smiled innocently. 'England Manager. Sir.'

Ramsey raised his eyebrows. 'Could be worse,' he growled. 'Although we made a bad defensive error to allow their goal.'

'Just a blip though, wasn't it?' said Rory encouragingly. 'I wouldn't worry. I'm sure your back four will play an absolute blinder for the rest of the match.'

'You think so?'

'I do, sir. I *know* so. Trust me.'

A crazy idea suddenly popped into Rory's head. After the many hours he had spent playing *FIFA* and *Football Manager*, he liked to think he knew a thing or two about getting the best out of a team, and here was the only opportunity he was ever likely to have to influence a real soccer manager. And not just *any* manager. The most famous English coach in history.

'I wonder, Mr Ramsey, sir . . . might I make a suggestion?'

'Go on.'

'It's just . . . well, watching the first half, sir, it crossed my mind that we might give their centre-backs a bit more trouble if you told Ball to use that near-post cross of his more. He's on fire today.'

Ramsey fixed Rory with a severe look for a few unnerving moments. Rory was beginning to realise that the English manager didn't really do other kinds of looks.

'Interesting suggestion,' said Ramsey at last. 'You might even have a point. Now, if you'll excuse me, I have a World Cup team to coach. And as for you, young man, you'd best get out of here.'

Rory hastily stepped aside, with an awkward half bow. He watched Ramsey move away towards the players' tunnel, and let out a huge sigh of relief. That had been a *very* close shave. And what was he thinking, giving the England manager tactical tips?

He ducked back inside the changing room and quickly twisted the dial casing on the shimmer to reactivate it. The now-familiar sickening ache gripped his stomach. He glanced across at the mirror above the sink – and saw Tofiq Bahramov staring palely back at him.

Daring to delay no further, Rory dived back out into the corridor and hurried after Ramsey, ready – or as ready as he would ever be – for the second half.

Chapter 12

Bomb Scare

'Nearly there, Pond!' puffed the Doctor. 'Just up ahead, on the left!'

The Doctor and Amy were running back along the stadium corridor. It was the one they had followed earlier, which led past the room where they had spied the Jules Rimet Trophy.

'There's someone coming out!' said Amy. 'Look!'

They came to a standstill. Twenty metres along the corridor, a group of four police officers had just emerged through the press-room door. They were the men who earlier had been guarding the trophy. One of them had it with him now, carrying it carefully in its glass case. The police party began making its way in the opposite direction from Amy and the Doctor.

'Excuse me! Hello there!'

All four officers looked round in surprise at the

Doctor's shout. As he quickly strode forward to join them, he slipped his hand into his inside jacket pocket. He muttered a quiet aside to Amy. 'About time you and I had a career change, don't you think, Pond? Been with FOOFA long enough.' He pulled out his psychic paper. 'How do you fancy being a plain-clothes police officer?'

Amy snorted. 'There's nothing plain about your clothes, Mr Braces and Bow Tie,' she whispered back.

'Hello, hello!' said the Doctor cheerily, as he and Amy approached. He grinned. 'Or should that be 'ello, 'ello, 'ello?' He hooked his thumbs in his braces, and bent both knees to bob up and down.

The four police officers glared at him. Not one showed even a trace of a smile.

'Just kidding. You know. Classic bobby-on-the-beat thing,' persevered the Doctor, still smiling. 'No?'

The nearest police officer stepped forward. The shoulders of his uniform bore the triple chevrons of a sergeant. He was clearly in charge.

'How can we help you, sir?' The sergeant's tone was rather severe.

'The name's Lineker. Agent Lineker,' replied the Doctor. 'From Metropolitan Special Branch.' He held out his psychic paper for inspection.

The sergeant peered at it warily.

'This is my colleague, Agent Beckham.' The Doctor gestured to Amy. She gave the officers a solemn nod.

The sergeant's suspicious gaze was still fixed on the psychic paper. Finally he looked back at the Doctor.

'You're with Special Branch?' he said, raising his eyebrows.

'Indeed, sergeant. Plain clothes.'

Amy cleared her throat.

'And what can we do for you, Agent Lineker?' asked the sergeant.

The Doctor extended one of his long fingers. 'I'd be terribly grateful if I could borrow that trophy you've got there.'

The sergeant frowned. 'Can't let you do that, sir, I'm afraid. I'm under strict orders to see that it gets to the Royal Box safely. Her Majesty is to present it at the end of the match. I was told not to let it out of my sight. I'm sure you understand, sir – after the recent theft, and all.'

The Doctor tucked away his psychic paper, then clapped a hand on the sergeant's shoulder. 'Absolutely, sergeant. And you won't have to. Let it out of your sight, I mean. I just need to take a quick look at it. But it is rather important that I examine the cup *before* it comes into the Queen's proximity.'

'And why would that be, sir?'

'Because, sergeant, we have reason to believe it's a bomb.'

All four police officers looked understandably alarmed.

'A bomb?' the sergeant echoed.

'That's right. As you say, the trophy went missing recently. Special Branch has been looking into exactly who took it. We've just uncovered evidence that it was stolen – and then returned – by a known anti-royal terrorist. One Rory "The Wrecker" Williams. Very nasty piece of work. Show them, Beckham.'

Amy was caught a little off guard. She hastily dug out her mobile phone, and used its touchscreen to open up her photo library. She filtered the library for images of Rory. It didn't take her long to find a pretty grim head-and-shoulders photo of him. Boy, did she remember *that* party . . . Amy selected the photo for full-screen display and held up her phone for the sergeant to see.

All four officers had watched the entire process open-mouthed. None of them had ever dreamt of, let alone seen, technology like this. To the 1960s mind, Amy's twenty-first century phone was about as jaw-dropping as pure magic. Which, Amy realised, was precisely why the Doctor had suggested she use it. In the eyes of the four police officers, such incredible

technology could only have been issued by Special
Branch. They now bought the Doctor's story hook,
line and sinker.

'Williams is a genius with explosives,' the Doctor
continued. 'And he has something against the Royal
Family. We've already foiled one attempt on Prince
Philip's life. Rigged polo saddle. Nasty business. We
believe Williams has booby-trapped the World Cup
trophy, knowing that it's to be presented by Her
Majesty.'

'Really, sir?' The sergeant was gripped now. 'We
can't have that, sir.'

'No, sergeant, we can't,' agreed the Doctor
earnestly. 'So if I could just take a quick look . . .'

At the sergeant's signal, the officer holding the
cased trophy hurriedly passed it to the Doctor. The
constable looked rather relieved. He had been a little
fidgety ever since the mention of the word 'bomb'.

'Now then . . .' muttered the Doctor, placing the
case gently on the corridor floor.

He took out his sonic screwdriver, then knelt
down to apply it to the lock on the case's lid. The
lock immediately released. The four officers looked
on in amazement. This lock-cracking gadget was
obviously another piece of Special Branch
techno-wizardry.

The Doctor lifted the heavy trophy from the case. He began scanning its golden surface with his sonic screwdriver's glowing green tip.

He turned the trophy over. As he did so, it momentarily slipped in his grasp. All four police officers flinched visibly. The Doctor grinned at them. 'Whoops!'

He turned his attention to the roughly cubic block of lapis lazuli that formed the base of the trophy. As he scanned its underside, the sonic flickered more brightly.

'A-ha!' The Doctor fiddled with the sonic screwdriver's controls, then applied it once more to the exact centre of the lapis lazuli. Very slowly, he began to draw the sonic's tip away.

Amy watched in amazement. Something thin and pale pink was gradually emerging from the trophy's base, as though drawn out by the pull of the sonic. It was a spiralling filament covered in tiny frill-like swirls. It was made of a translucent, coral-coloured material. In fact, that was what it most reminded Amy of – coral. A long, slender spiral of fragile coral.

'What's that?' she asked, before thinking.

The Doctor flashed her a look. He carefully drew out another few centimetres of the whatever-it-was. Its end finally emerged from the trophy base, leaving no trace of a hole. The Doctor caught it as it came free and passed it to Amy.

'High-explosive strand, Beckham,' he said gravely, with a discreet wink. 'As we suspected. Complete with detonator. Very hi-tech. This Williams monster knows his stuff.' The Doctor stood up and tucked his sonic screwdriver back in his pocket. 'There! All done!'

Without warning, he casually tossed the trophy towards the police officer who had originally held it. Fortunately, the constable had good reactions. He caught the hefty gold cup, staring at it like it was a live grenade.

'No need to worry!' the Doctor reassured him. 'It won't harm anyone now! Completely defused. You can pop it back in its case and get it over to the Royal Box for the presentation as planned.' He turned to the sergeant. 'And I'd appreciate it if we could keep this little incident to ourselves, yes? National security, and all that. Come, Agent Beckham!' He gestured to the nearby open doorway. 'You and I have important Special Branch-type things to discuss.'

'Right.' Amy nodded. 'Absolutely.' She led the way into the press room, still holding the strange coral-like strand.

The Doctor gave the four dumbstruck police officers a final broad smile, then followed Amy, closing the door behind him.

There was a long silence in the corridor.

'Sarge?' The youngest officer was first to speak. 'How hard is it to get into Special Branch?'

Chapter 13
The Big Problem

'So, Agent Lineker, what does this thing really do?'

Amy was examining the peculiar coral-like filament that the Doctor had just extracted from the base of the Jules Rimet Trophy. The two of them were alone in the press room.

'It's a displacement anchor,' replied the Doctor. 'Acts as both a beacon and a fixing point for the Vispic larvae. It's what's calling them all here to Wembley. And it serves as a secure anchorage once they get here.'

'You make it sound like they're having to cling on.'

'They are, in a way. Displacing yourself isn't easy. There are strong forces acting to keep you at your point of origin. The Vispics can override those forces if they have a sufficiently secure displacement anchor to fix on to in their target location – and that's exactly what you're holding.'

'But where did it come from?'

'The first Vispic to burrow a wormhole into Earth space must have managed to do so unassisted. Probably the one that turned into the larger adult we saw. It must have set up that anchor so that others could follow.'

'But it was inside the World Cup,' said Amy. 'I mean, that's a bit weird, isn't it? Why there?'

'Think about it, Amy,' said the Doctor. 'What better place could there be? By its very nature, the trophy is always a focus for celebration and joy. Winning the World Cup creates mass euphoria among the fans of the winning nation. And the trophy is at the heart of that upsurge of good feeling – exactly where a hungry, luck-sucking larva would choose to be.' The Doctor settled on the edge of the table. 'Rory's whole trophy-theft story struck me as odd right away. Why did the cup turn up again? Any thief capable of stealing it in the first place would hardly have been so inept as to leave it lying in a hedge. Unless of course they *intended* it to be recovered . . .'

Amy didn't look like she was keeping up.

The Doctor went on. 'The police never did manage to track down the culprit. But then they were looking for a human . . .'

The penny dropped. 'You mean – that adult Vispic

took it?' Amy looked at the filament. 'To put this inside?'

The Doctor nodded. 'I don't wish to take any credit away from our canine hero Pickles, but it was part of the Vispic plan that the trophy should be found. It was a simple way to ensure the trophy returned to the centre of World Cup activity with the displacement anchor concealed inside.'

The Doctor put out a hand for the anchor. Amy passed it to him. He took out his sonic screwdriver and gave the filament a quick once-over.

'Their plan's worked a treat, too, hasn't it?' said Amy grimly. 'All those larvae under the stands, ready and waiting for the fans to go crazy so they can suck all the happiness out of them.'

'Don't throw in the towel just yet, Pond!' The Doctor tucked his sonic away and slid off the tabletop. He began pacing the floor, twirling the strange frilled strand like a majorette's baton. 'This thing may be the reason so many Vispics have found their way here, but it might also offer us a way of sending them packing.'

'How?'

'As I said, there are forces that act to resist an organism displacing itself. A strong pull back towards the point of origin – a bit like being attached to where you set off from by a piece of elastic. While the Vispics have a secure anchor point –' he waggled the filament at her – 'they can withstand that pull. But if we were to *destroy* it . . .'

'*Twang!*' cried Amy excitedly.

'Exactly. No more Vispics. The whole host of larvae and adults would be instantly drawn back to their original location.'

The Doctor stopped pacing, held up the filament, and stared at it searchingly. 'This is the key to the Vispics' scheme, but also its weakness. Another reason, I imagine, why they hid it so well.'

'So what are we waiting for?' asked Amy. 'Let's smash it up!'

'Be my guest.'

The Doctor tossed the filament back to Amy. She took hold of it by its ends, and attempted to snap it in two. She gritted her teeth and tried harder. But, despite its fragile appearance, the slim strand wouldn't break.

Amy decided to get serious. She dragged a table across from against the press-room wall and positioned it next to the one in the centre of the room, leaving a narrow gap between them. Then she laid the filament across the gap. She picked up a sturdy wooden chair, lifted it over her head, and brought it crashing down.

The chair disintegrated, splintering into a twisted

mess. Amy yelled as the jolt jarred her upper body. She dropped what was left of the chair. The filament lay on the floor, entirely undamaged.

Amy glared at the Doctor, red-faced. 'I'm not going to be able to break it, am I?'

The Doctor shook his head.

'You knew that already, didn't you?' said Amy.

The Doctor nodded. He reached down to pick up the displacement anchor. He closed one eye and squinted along its length, first from one end, then the other.

'That, Pond, is our big problem. How to unmake it. It appears to be built around a molecular core of Paratraxium. Almost indestructible.'

'Almost?'

The Doctor hesitated.

'I can think of two ways in which it *might* be destroyed,' he told Amy.

'Go on.'

'The first would involve subjecting it to a very high temperature. The sort generated near the Earth's core, or at the heart of an erupting volcano.'

'Not a great option, that one, is it?' said Amy drily. 'I'm guessing there's not a lot of volcanic activity in north-west London right now. What's Plan B?'

'To run a powerful electric pulse through it,' said

the Doctor. 'Paratraxium has an extremely high electrical resistance. If the voltage was sufficient, it should cause the core to heat up beyond its tolerance.'

'Now you're talking. Electricity we have – even in the sixties.'

'Not at the sort of voltage we'd need. It would take over a hundred thousand volts. No part of London's city grid carries that sort of flow.'

'Isn't there any other way?'

The Doctor shook his head.

Amy wasn't having it. 'There must be *something* we can do!' she insisted. 'We can't just sit around and wait for half the population of London to go down the tube . . .'

The Doctor's face lit up. He seized Amy by the shoulders.

'Pond, you're a genius! You've done it again!'

'What?' Amy looked confused.

'That's the answer! The Tube!' cried the Doctor. 'The London Underground! The whole track is electrified!'

'You think we might be able to fry this thing by hooking it up to a Tube line?'

'Not directly, no. The electrified track probably carries about a thousand volts of direct current, at most. One kilovolt isn't enough. But there must be some way to amplify it . . .'

The Doctor began pacing back and forth once more, running his hands through his hair as he tried to think.

'Wembley's entire roof is supported on an aluminium framework. I might be able to multi-loop the electric flow through that. Create a makeshift step-up transformer. Boost the voltage. We'd need to run it through an inverter first, to get an alternating current . . .'

The Doctor was taking shorter and shorter circuits.

'It *could* work! If I get the roof-loop right, we should be able to create a powerful enough electric pulse to disintegrate the Paratraxium core!'

'Then bye-bye, Luck-suckers!' said Amy. 'Brilliant!'

'I'd have to isolate the stands themselves, of course . . .'

'Or?'

'Or ninety-three thousand football fans will get a nasty shock,' said the Doctor. 'Literally.'

Amy looked concerned. 'Okay . . . feeling *slightly* less enthusiastic now.'

'And it'll take me a little while to set up.' He stopped pacing and looked at Amy, his eyes alive. 'I'll need *you* to make the connection to the Underground system.'

'Course you will. And that'll involve more running, presumably?'

'Possibly a little, Pond,' admitted the Doctor. He flashed her a grin. 'But probably a lot.'

Chapter 14

Come On, England!

Out on the Wembley pitch, both teams were giving it everything they had. There were only three or four minutes of normal time left to play. England were a goal up.

The teams had been locked in a 1–1 stalemate for most of the gruelling second half. Then, in the seventy-eighth minute, England had finally broken the deadlock. They had snatched a crucial second goal. It had come from an Alan Ball cross – much to Rory's delight. Ball had delivered his corner-kick to Hurst, whose deflected shot had fallen kindly for his West Ham teammate Martin Peters.

As Peters' close-range shot had hit the back of the German net, Rory had let out a triumphant whoop. A split second later, he had remembered who he was supposed to be – a neutral, unbiased official. He had hastily tried to disguise his delighted reaction as a fit of energetic coughing.

He needn't have bothered. The watching fans weren't interested in the linesman's rather peculiar behaviour. They were too busy either screaming their heads off with delight, or hanging them in despair.

Since then, West Germany had been doing everything in their power to save the match. A goal down, with time running out, they had pushed everyone forward. They were mounting attack after attack on the English goal.

But England, too, were digging deep. The players were defending valiantly, determined not to concede a goal. They knew that a famous victory was within their reach. The World Cup would be theirs if they could hold on for just a few more minutes . . .

The English fans in the packed stands were in an agony of expectation. One moment they were cheering wildly as Nobby Stiles made yet another vital tackle; the next they were gasping with relief as Gordon Banks just managed to punch away a fierce German shot. The trophy was *so* nearly in their grasp . . .

No one was more on edge than Rory. He was finding the suspense almost as unbearable as the stomach-churning effect of the shimmer. He was beginning to regret wishing that history should follow its familiar course. That would mean the match going into extra time – another thirty minutes of play. Rory wasn't sure he could hold it together that long.

Maybe the Germans won't equalise, he thought hopefully.

Despite his many TARDIS trips, Rory still struggled with the whole reliving-history thing. Time travel did his head in – particularly going *back* in time. Was it inevitable that events on the pitch would follow the pattern he knew, or not? Perhaps a straightforward 2–1 win for England was still a possibility. Maybe this time round, there would be no extra time, no controversial goal-line decision to make.

Another tremendous roar went up from the crowd as Banks claimed the ball from a dangerous German cross. The England goalkeeper was playing out of his skin.

The crowd had been brilliant. The rousing support from the England fans had been constant throughout the match. The atmosphere was fantastic. No one was crazier for football than the English.

It struck Rory – not for the first time – as a great shame that England hadn't hosted a World Cup in his lifetime. He knew that during the time he had been travelling with the Doctor the Football Association had tried to bring the tournament to English turf. He had pinned his hopes on their bid to stage the 2018 tournament, but it hadn't come off. Wembley wouldn't see another match like this in a very long time.

Rory's thoughts were brought back to the here and now by another loud outburst from the crowd. This time, it was a collective groan from the England fans. The referee had awarded West Germany a free kick, just outside the English penalty box. Jack Charlton had been penalised for a foul on the German captain, Seeler.

The match was now into its final minute. But there was still time for the Germans to ruin the English party.

The teams had changed ends for the second half, which meant the English goal was now at the opposite end of the pitch to Rory. He watched anxiously from a distance, as West German winger Lothar Emmerich lined up to take the kick. The volume of the crowd's cheers fell dramatically, as thousands of English fans held their breath.

Rory remembered this free kick only too well. It looked like history was about to repeat – or replay – itself after all.

Sure enough, moments later, Wolfgang Weber was streaking away from the English goal, arms held aloft in celebration. Emmerich's kick had been bravely blocked, but the deflected ball had fallen for Weber, who was rushing in at the far post. His close-range shot had given Banks no chance. The Germans had equalised within the dying seconds of normal time.

Rory glumly looked up at the scoreboard. It was mounted on a rather precarious-looking balcony, jutting out from under the stadium's west-end roof to Rory's right. It showed the team names and scores in white text on a black background. Two men in white coats were perched on the gallery that ran behind it. It was their job to manually change the giant numerals that made up the scoreline display.

Rory watched one of the scoreboard officials replace the 1 next to GERMANY W. with a large 2 – and heard the referee's whistle blow for the end of normal time. He looked over his shoulder at the North Stand, which had fallen very quiet. The England fans were looking shell-shocked, stunned by this last-gasp German goal. Rory looked across row upon row of dismayed faces. Then he did a double-take. For a moment, he was almost sure he had caught sight of a figure running across the North Stand roof. A very familiar figure.

Rory shook his head to clear it. The shimmer must have been messing with his vision. He looked up again.

No, there was nobody up there. His eyes were playing tricks.

Why would the Doctor have been on the roof anyway?

Rory turned his attention back to the pitch. The England and West Germany players were making the most of the short interval before extra time, taking the opportunity to rest and stretch. They would be hoping to stave off cramp and somehow coax another thirty minutes of running time out of their tired legs.

I've got to hang in there too, thought Rory determinedly. He mustn't let his concentration falter now, however grim the shimmer was making him feel. Once extra time kicked off, he would need to be on his toes. His big moment – Hurst's controversial second goal – was fast approaching.

And if I don't get things exactly right in the next thirty minutes, he thought anxiously, *it could all be over for England.*

Though Rory could not have known it, at that very moment, up on the North Stand roof, the Doctor was thinking exactly the same thing.

Chapter 15
The Wrong TARDIS

Amy sprinted north along Olympic Way, her heart pounding. For the umpteenth time since leaving the stadium, she checked over her shoulder. She couldn't shake the feeling that someone – or something – was following her. But, as far as she could tell, she was still alone.

She didn't slacken her pace, though. Even if she wasn't being pursued – for a change – she was still up against the clock. The Doctor's plan would only work if they could put it into action before the Vispic larvae transformed. Which meant they only had until the end of the match. Time was running out fast.

Amy reached the junction with Fulton Road and turned right on to its south-side pavement. The main road, which had been so busy earlier, was now deserted. Her route along Olympic Way had been eerily quiet too. Anyone who wasn't actually at the match was tucked away inside somewhere, following it on the radio – or, if they were lucky enough to have access to one, watching it on TV. London's streets had never been so empty.

Amy jogged along the pavement, then crossed to the other side of the road again. She passed the news stand where she, Rory and the Doctor had stopped off earlier. It was locked up and unattended.

She was beginning to get a stitch. But it wasn't far now. Albion Way, where the TARDIS had materialised, was just up ahead. She put on a final effort to keep up her speed, determined not to let the Doctor down . . .

PC Sanderson's good intentions of listening to just some of the match hadn't quite worked out – the game was now in its ninetieth minute, and the policeman was still shut away in his call box, listening intently to the gripping commentary on his borrowed radio.

'. . . *and as Emmerich strides forward to take this last-ditch free kick, a nervous silence has fallen over the England fans* . . .'

'Miss it, miss it, miss it,' muttered Sanderson. He was perched on the edge of the box's bench seat, with a forgotten cup of tea cold in his hand.

114

'*Emmerich's shot is blocked by Cohen and – oh! Dear me! It's a goal! Weber scores for Germany!*'

'No!' Sanderson let out a groan of despair and slumped back against the wall of the box.

'*There are appeals from the English players for handball! But the referee waves away their protests! The goal stands. The West German centre-back has snatched a last-minute equaliser . . .*'

Sanderson couldn't believe what he was hearing. How could England have let West Germany score now, when they were so close to victory?

' *. . . and there's the whistle to signal the end of the second half! So, it's all square at two-all. Both teams will need to summon the energy to play another thirty minutes to decide this epic contest. England, who only moments ago seemed destined to lift the World Cup here at Wembley, now find themselves still with everything to do to win th–*'

Suddenly Sanderson stood bolt upright, spilling his tea. Someone had just burst through the door of the police box.

It was a pretty young woman with long red hair. She was breathing fast. She looked as surprised to see Sanderson as he was to see her.

'Ah . . .' She looked around the box's cramped interior as though it wasn't what she had expected to find. 'Sorry . . . my . . . mistake . . .' she panted. 'Wrong TARDIS!'

She took another second or two to get her breath. Sanderson was still too taken aback to speak.

The stranger flashed a smile at him. 'Sorry if I startled you, officer.' She glanced at the radio set, which was still chattering away. 'Been following the match?'

Sanderson looked a little sheepish. 'I was . . . erm . . . just listening to a few minutes, yes, miss.'

'How's it going?'

'Not well. It looked like we had it won, but the Germans just equalised. It's going to extra time.'

The young woman looked delighted. 'Yes!'

Sanderson frowned. He failed to see how Germany scoring could be good news. 'But surely you don't want Germany to win?'

'No,' said the redhead. 'No, I don't want Germany to win. I don't want anyone to win just yet. Extra time is absolutely what we need.'

Sanderson was finding this unexpected conversation increasingly confusing. He decided to start again. 'May I ask your name, miss?'

'You go first.'

'Very well. PC Sanderson of Harlesden Police Station at your service.'

'First name?'

'William. Bill.'

This wasn't going as Sanderson had intended. Somehow, he seemed to have ended up answering the questions.

'Bill.' The girl smiled. 'As in "the old Bill". Good name for a copper. That and Bobby.'

Sanderson once again tried to take charge. 'And you are?'

In response, the young woman pulled a slim, shiny rectangular object from her pocket. She stared at its smooth surface for a moment, stroking and tapping it several times with her finger. Sanderson was amazed to see tiny luminous pictures flit across the device's glassy face. The girl held it up in front of him.

'Agent Beckham, Special Branch.'

Sanderson stared in disbelief. It was a miniature display screen, not altogether unlike a tiny television. It showed a picture of the redhead's face, with the text MY PROFILE above it. There was more text underneath, but before he could read it the young woman withdrew her hand.

'What . . . what *is* that thing?' stammered Sanderson. 'It's amazing!'

'Standard-issue Special Branch equipment.'

'So, you're with the Met? Like me?'

'Uh-huh. But plain clothes, assigned to anti-terrorist stuff.' She moved closer to address him earnestly. 'We have a serious situation on our hands, PC Bill Sanderson. A Code Thirteen.'

'Code Thirteen?'

'Extraterrestrial invasion,' stated the young woman without flinching. 'How do you fancy helping to save the population of London, Bill?'

'Extraterrestrial inva—' Sanderson pulled a face. 'Is this some kind of joke, miss?'

The young woman's expression didn't falter. She was deadly serious, he could see.

'You're suggesting . . . aliens?' said Sanderson. 'But that's not possible!' He hesitated. 'Is it?' The magical technology the young constable had just seen in action had turned his idea of what was possible upside down. 'I mean, they don't exist, do they?'

'Oh, yeah. They exist all right. And right now they're out and about here in London. Big scary people-eating ones. I could use a little help dealing with them.'

Sanderson was finding this surprise meeting most unsettling. Once more, he tried to get a grip. 'You say you're from Special Branch?'

The young woman nodded.

'Were they behind setting up that second call box?' asked Sanderson. 'The one next to this one? Has that got something to do with all this?'

Agent Beckham's eyes lit up. 'It *has*, Sanderson. Smart guess. And a quick look inside there should change your mind about the whole "impossible" thing.' She turned back towards the open door. 'Come on – I'll show you around.'

The bewildered police officer found the idea of being shown around a five-square-foot box slightly odd – but, then again, everything about this meeting had been odd. Deciding to save his questions for the time being, he followed the young woman out through the call-box door and then into the other box alongside.

Amy watched PC Sanderson's face as he struggled to take in his surroundings. She remembered her own reaction to the TARDIS's mind-bending interior the first time she had seen it. Sanderson was going through the same sequence of emotions – total shock, shifting to amazed delight, then on to utter bafflement.

'But . . .' His voice trailed off. He continued to gawp uncomprehendingly at the vast, cavernous interior of the Time Lord craft.

Amy grinned at him. 'Loopy, isn't it? Bet you never realised Special Branch was *that* special!'

She hurried up the ramp towards the central circular platform, then made her way round the console to her left, peering down at the floor.

'Now then . . . third segment round, clockwise, from the ramp. That's what the Doctor said. One . . . two . . . three!' She dropped to her knees beside a rectangular panel in the floor. 'Top-left corner . . .' muttered Amy, reaching across it. She made a fist and gave the floor a good hard thump. The opposite ends of the panel suddenly seemed to shrink back slightly, and its surface became scored with narrow concertina folds. Amy slipped her hand into the gap that had appeared at one edge. She slid the panel aside to reveal a crammed storage hatch below.

Amy hastily began rummaging through the hatch's contents. She lifted out a strange contraption that looked like someone had covered a small fire extinguisher with sink-plunger suction cups. Amy laid it to one side, then fished out another equally bizarre-looking piece of equipment. Then another. And another.

'Who's the Doctor?' Sanderson was still staring about, wide-eyed, but he had regained the ability to speak.

'Er, a fellow Special Branch officer,' Amy replied without leaving off her search. 'Agent Lineker. What is *that*?' She impatiently cast aside yet another peculiar device. 'He's running this operation. The Doctor is sort of a code name.'

'Right.' The constable nodded numbly.

'He's our Code Thirteen expert,' Amy went on. 'Knows loads about aliens and stuff.'

'I see.'

As she drew her next find from the hatch, Amy gave a triumphant cry. 'Gotcha!'

She was holding a pair of very large crocodile clips, locked together by their sprung jaws. They had handle-grips made of colourful rubbery material. Both had one red handle and one yellow.

Amy got to her feet, and hurried back down the ramp.

'What are they?' asked PC Sanderson.

'Connectors. Together they're a cordless extension lead, apparently. The Doctor – Agent Lineker, I mean – thinks they might help us with the save-the-city thing.'

'How?'

Amy made for the TARDIS door. 'I'll explain on the way.'

'Where?'

Sanderson followed her back out on to the pavement of Albion Way. He was beginning to feel embarrassed by his one-word questions.

'Wembley Park Tube station,' Amy told him. 'We need to get there as fast as possible – which is where I was hoping you might be able to help. Do you have a bicycle I could use?'

'Not a pedal bike, no,' said Sanderson. 'But I could take you there on the back of my patrol bike.'

He quickly led Amy round the back of his own police box. Parked against the kerb was a gleaming black motorcycle. It was a 650cc Triumph Thunderbird, the standard patrol bike of the Metropolitan force and Sanderson's pride and joy.

'Would that do?' he asked.

Amy looked at the immaculate motorcycle admiringly. It was a truly classic machine. As a teenager, Amy had had a poster on her bedroom wall of a young Marlon Brando – in her opinion the most gorgeous male movie star of all time – that had been taken from the film *The Wild One*, and showed Brando sitting astride a bike just like this one.

Amy gave Sanderson a broad grin.

'Absolutely, constable,' she purred. 'That'll do very nicely indeed.'

Chapter 16
Goalsky!

Rory checked his watch. Not the fake Vinvocci wristwatch – which he was beginning to hate with all his heart – but his own, ordinary, non-stomach-churning one.

Nine minutes of extra time were almost up. Rory knew Geoff Hurst would score his controversial goal in the eleventh minute. That meant he had a little over sixty seconds before his big moment arrived. Then it would be up to him to make sure the vital goal counted.

To his horror, Rory suddenly realised that so far he had given no thought as to how he would communicate his decision that the goal should stand. He knew from watching old TV footage of the famous match that after Hurst's shot the referee came running over to the touchline to consult Bahramov. What was he going to do when that happened?

Should he have prepared something to say? In Azerbaijani?

Presumably Bahramov must have said something like 'Yes, it was a goal' when the referee asked his opinion – even if the Swiss official didn't understand the linesman's exact words.

But what on Earth was that in Azerbaijani?

Rory's mind raced. His knowledge of the Azerbaijani language was non-existent, and his grasp of Russian was barely better. What little Russian he knew he had picked up from watching old spy films, which often had a Russian character as the criminal mastermind. Rory recalled a scene in an early James Bond movie in which a cold-hearted Russian villain refused to listen to reason. What did the baddie say as he shook his head mercilessly?

Nyet – that was it. So *nyet* was *no*. But what was *yes*?

Rory tried to picture the same Bond villain giving orders to his band of armed heavies. What was it they grunted as they nodded obediently?

Da. Of course! *Yes* was *da*, he was sure.

As for the 'it was a goal' bit, he would just have to wing it. If he made up some Russian-sounding words, maybe the referee wouldn't notice they weren't genuine. A lot of Russian names ended in *-ov* or *-sky*, didn't they? He could include a few of those endings in whatever he said . . .

Rory's attention was drawn back to the game. Alan Ball had just sprinted past just in front of him, chasing the ball down the right wing. Rory could see the two English centre-forwards, Hurst and Hunt, hurrying forward in support. He recognised the shape of this attacking move from the many, many times he had seen these particular seconds of play before – and knew the time for planning was over.

This was it.

Ball whipped in a short cross to the near side of the German penalty box. Hurst had found space to receive it. He controlled the ball with his first touch, then spun towards the goal and fired in a fierce, rising shot. It rocketed over the flat-capped head of the West German keeper, Hans Tilkowski.

The ball hit the midpoint of the crossbar, hard. It ricocheted off the underside of the bar, straight downward, and struck the ground between the German goalposts.

The deflection off the bar had set the ball spinning fiercely. The spin caused it to bounce up at an angle, out of the goalmouth. A desperate German defender headed the ball over his own goal to put it out of play.

But the English players were already celebrating. They ran to congratulate Hurst, convinced that his shot had crossed the goal line, and that he had just put them ahead.

The West Germans felt otherwise. Rory watched them surround the referee, protesting. The Swiss official waved them away, then began to make his way across the pitch towards Rory.

One thing Rory had never expected was that, when the time came, he would be in any doubt as to whether he was doing the fair thing. To his own astonishment, after witnessing the Hurst goal first-hand, he was a tiny bit uneasy. He felt a twinge of guilt that he was about to try his best to make sure the goal stood. In truth, it really didn't look like the ball had completely crossed the line . . .

Then he remembered the 2010 Frank Lampard no-goal, and his moment of madness passed. He was doing this for his country. For England. And for Frank.

The referee was now hurrying towards him. Heart pounding in his chest, Rory strode forward on to the pitch to meet him. The referee fixed him with an urgent, enquiring look and said something in German. From his expression and body language, it was clearly along the lines of 'What do you think?'

Rory went for it.

'Da! Da! Goalsky!' He concentrated hard on doing his best (not great) Russian accent. 'Da! Goalsky!' He threw in some very earnest nodding and finger-wagging. 'Nyet problemov! Goalsky! Da! Da!'

It worked. The referee seemed to get the vital message loud and clear. He showed no sign of suspecting that his linesman was an impostor – let alone a non-Russian-speaking twenty-first century time traveller disguised by an alien shape-changing device. He simply nodded back at Rory, then raised an arm and gave a shrill blast on his whistle. The goal had been awarded.

As the referee turned and jogged back towards the centre spot, Rory felt a flood of relief. He was only vaguely aware of the several West German players who came rushing up seconds later to confront him. He knew as little German as he did Russian, but he was pretty sure from the players' angry expressions that they weren't saying thank you.

He didn't care. He'd done it. The score was now 3–2 to England, like it had always been meant to be.

The match was quickly restarted from the centre spot. As Rory watched the two teams continue to fight it out, he could clearly see how much the Hurst goal had lifted the spirits of the English players. They looked revitalised and resolute.

Despite his aching stomach and throbbing head, Rory was glad he'd stepped into the missing linesman's shoes. Watching the England players pass the ball about confidently, he was more convinced than ever that the Bahramov decision was a crucial turning point in the match. Now, surely, England ought to be safely on their way to their famous victory.

Nevertheless, as the match moved into the second period of extra time, Rory awaited the final whistle just as anxiously as did the many millions of his countrymen watching with him.

Come on, England . . .

Chapter 17
A Shocking Encounter

Amy took the steps down to the platform three at a
time. She had left the indignant ticket attendant in the
capable hands of PC Sanderson. The constable was
even now calmly explaining to the man why Amy had
just jumped the barrier. As she sprinted away, Amy
had heard him speaking earnestly of 'police business'
and 'national security'.

She bounded down the last few steps and dashed on
to the platform. Although Wembley Park station was
part of the London Underground network, it was not
actually underground. The train tracks here ran in the
open air, as they did in many outer parts of the city.

A northbound Metropolitan Line train was just

pulling out of the nearest platform. *Perfect.* That should mean she'd have a little time before the next train was due.

Amy hurried to the platform's edge and quickly lowered herself down on to the track. Fortunately, the station was deserted. There were no well-meaning bystanders to attempt to stop her. Most Londoners were following the big match, no doubt – blissfully unaware that the final whistle might signal the end of London life as they knew it.

Amy took a good look at the track, wondering where best to make the connection. There were three rails as there were on all Underground tracks. The outer two were for the carriage wheels to run on, while the middle rail carried the electricity that powered the trains – enough electricity to kill her, Amy knew, if she accidentally touched the rail.

She turned to lay one of the two crocodile-clip connectors on the platform edge. Holding the other, she stepped over the near-side rail, then carefully crouched down over the central electrified one.

Gotta get this right . . . she thought anxiously. If she fastened the connector in the wrong place, it would simply be knocked off by the next train. That wouldn't do.

But if I clip it on from underneath . . .

Amy squeezed the insulated handles of the connector together, and very gingerly clamped its jaws to the underside of the electrified rail. Her hand was shaking a little – but not enough, thankfully, to make contact with the rail.

She twisted the red handle of the connector, as the Doctor had told her, to activate it. Then she carefully released her grip. The connector stayed clamped in place, tucked out of the way of any passing wheels and more or less out of sight. So far so good.

Amy had been so intent on avoiding electrocution that she had failed to notice that the two outer rails were giving off a faint whistling hum. She heard it now. The hum was quickly growing louder.

There was a train coming.

Amy fought against her fatal instinct to freeze with fear. Instead, she sprang back over the near-side rail and hauled herself up over the platform's edge. As she rolled away from it, a blast of air and noise rushed over her. A silvery blur rattled past – another A-Stock Metropolitan Line train pulling into the station.

As the train gradually slowed, Amy got to her feet and brushed herself down. She felt more than a little shaky. She had narrowly missed plenty of trains before, but she had never had one narrowly miss her.

She bent down to pick up the second connector.

According to the Doctor, twisting this one's red handle would channel a current from the electrical source to which its partner was attached. He had seemed confident that this cordless extension lead of his could carry the Tube track's kilovolt supply.

The newly arrived train drew at last to a halt. As it did so, Amy heard a clattering noise from the far end of the platform. It sounded very familiar. The eerie feeling that she wasn't alone came over her once more.

The train doors sliced open. Two passengers stepped out from the door nearest to Amy. A couple more disembarked from a carriage further along. Not many people were getting off. Just the four.

But that was enough.

Amy stared hard at the spot where she had heard the clattering a moment ago. A distinct area of seemingly empty space near the end of the platform had begun flickering unnaturally. Amy had little difficulty recognising its shape and size.

She had been right all along. One of the adult Vispics had followed her from the stadium. It had used its sophisticated camouflage to stay hidden. But now, in trying to conceal itself from more than one person, the creature had become partially visible.

Not for long. The handful of passengers were already heading up the steps towards the station's exit.

To her horror, Amy watched the flickering patch of air become still. The Vispic was once more focusing on her alone.

The clattering noise came again. This time it grew rapidly louder – and nearer. Amy backed away helplessly, sensing that the camouflaged creature was about to attack. A desperate idea sprang into her mind. She clutched the connector in both hands, thrust it out at arm's length and twisted the red handle.

The Doctor had warned Amy about the danger of activating the current. He had told her that she was not, on any account, to twist both red handles. A thousand volts could kill her stone dead.

Or save her skin.

The creature slammed into Amy just as she activated the connector. It got the shock of its life. As Amy sprawled backwards on to the platform, she kept firm hold of the connector's handles. A crackling web of white, lightning-like electricity leapt from the jaws of the connector and danced wildly around the outer surface of the Vispic's body.

The powerful jolt stunned the alien creature. It became fully visible. With an unearthly screech, it recoiled from Amy's improvised weapon. It collapsed clumsily on to its side on the platform, where it lay twitching, ribbons of white energy still skittering across its grotesque body.

Amy twisted the connector handle back again and hurriedly scrambled to her feet. She stared wide-eyed at the Vispic. It looked like the largest of the three that she and the Doctor had encountered under the South Stand. She wondered, for a moment, if she had killed it. But, even as she looked, the creature began to stir. The electric shock had stunned it – that was all.

Amy didn't hang around to wait for it to recover fully. She turned and sprinted for the stairs. She bounded up them towards the station exit, her pulse racing. Only at the top did she glance back over her shoulder.

The Vispic had vanished.

Amy put her head down and ran for her life.

Outside the Wembley Park station entrance, PC Sanderson was waiting anxiously on his patrol bike.

Agent Beckham – the red-haired whirlwind who had come ripping into his life and turned it upside down – had told him to be ready to make a hasty departure. She had spent the journey to the station with her arms wrapped tightly round him, yelling instructions in his ear over the growl of the Thunderbird's powerful engine. Once she'd done what she had to do at the Tube station, she'd explained, she needed him to get her to the Empire Stadium as fast as possible.

Sanderson smiled to himself. *Looks like I'm going to Wembley after all*, he thought.

To his surprise, he realised that he hadn't given the big match a thought for the last fifteen minutes or so. It had been driven from his mind by the fascinating stranger from Special Branch, with her sci-fi technology and talk of alien invaders.

And here she came now.

Sanderson saw her burst from the entrance of the Underground station. She was running like the Devil himself was after her and clutching just one of those giant crocodile clips she had brought with them.

At the sight of him, she gave a wild yell. 'Start your engine!'

Sanderson did as he was told. He stamped down on the Thunderbird's kick-starter, and the bike's engine roared into life. He shuffled forward on the leather saddle to make room for his pillion passenger.

But, before she could reach him, Agent Beckham stumbled and fell flat on her face. She had gone down as though something had caught her by the leg.

But there's nothing there . . .

Sanderson saw her twist on to her back. She thrust

135

the connector she was clinging to fiercely upward. A blaze of crackling electricity erupted from its tip. Sanderson was temporarily dazzled – but what he saw as the sparks faded made his heart falter.

Oh my . . .

Any remaining doubts about the young woman's alien-invasion story vanished from Sanderson's mind. A huge, hideous creature was lying on the pavement beside her. It had appeared out of nowhere. It was twitching horribly, its gross body sparking and smoking from the electric shock it had just sustained. But Sanderson could see that it was still undeniably alive.

He gunned the Thunderbird's engine. As its rear wheel spun, squealing, on the tarmac, he threw the bike's back end round. The motorcycle mounted the pavement and raced towards Agent Beckham, who was now struggling to her feet. Sanderson sent the bike into another sweeping skid so that its rear end came to a screeching halt right beside her.

'Jump on!'

As the young woman leapt astride the saddle behind him, Sanderson saw the alien thing begin to stir with more vigour. At close range, it was even more grotesque, and it was quickly recovering.

'Hold on tight!'

Agent Beckham didn't need telling twice. She wrapped her arms round Sanderson's waist and clung on. The young police officer opened up the motorbike's throttle.

The Thunderbird roared across Bridge Road, out on to Olympic Way and headed south towards Wembley.

Chapter 18
The Twin Towers

Amy's burning worry now was that she wouldn't reach
the Doctor in time. She had made the connection to
the electrified Tube rail. She was still in possession of
the second connector, which would allow the Doctor to
feed the Underground's supply into his voltage-boosting
device. But what if she and PC Sanderson couldn't find
him fast enough once they reached the stadium?

Amy knew there could be only minutes left before
the football match ended and the Vispic larvae would
begin to feast. Only minutes left to destroy the
displacement anchor and save London.

But finding the Doctor proved less of a problem
than Amy had feared. Only moments after PC
Sanderson brought his patrol bike to a skidding halt
outside the main stadium entrance and Amy had
quickly dismounted, she heard a familiar yell.

'Ahoy there, Amelia Pond! Glad you could make it!'

Amy looked up. She wasn't sure whether to feel relieved or horrified by what she saw. It was good to have found the Doctor so quickly, but what was he doing up there?

A thin silver wire stretched all the way from the flagpole on top of one of the stadium's twin white towers to the flagpole on the other. Halfway along it, dangling by one hand, was the Doctor. The Vispic displacement anchor was clasped in his other hand.

There was an alarming distance from the wire to the stadium roof below. Amy seriously hoped he knew what he was doing.

'I've got the extension lead!' she yelled back. She held the connector high so that the Doctor could see it. 'It's all plugged in, courtesy of London Transport!'

'Splendid work, Pond! Who's your friend?'

PC Sanderson had now also dismounted. He was standing beside Amy, gawping at the Doctor's daredevil high-wire act. He turned to look at her, puzzled.

'Amelia Pond?' That wasn't the name she had given him.

'Er . . .' Amy looked awkward. 'Yeah. It's . . . um . . . another Special Branch code name.' She hastily turned her attention back to the Doctor. 'This, Agent Lineker,' she yelled, 'is PC Sanderson. He got me back here in one piece!'

'Good man, Sanderson!' The Doctor now appeared to be attaching the displacement anchor to the midpoint of the wire with his free hand. A moment later, he let go of the slim filament. It stayed in place.

'Right! That's it! All set! We just need to connect up the juice!'

Amy and Sanderson watched anxiously as the Doctor began to make his way, hand over hand, along the wire and back towards the right-hand tower. He was almost halfway to the flagpole when he suddenly stopped.

'What's the matter, Doctor?' yelled Amy.

'Do me a favour, both of you!' he hollered back. 'Keep looking at that tower dome.'

Amy and Sanderson did as he asked: both fixed their eyes on the dome.

It took Amy a few seconds to see it. One area of the white dome was flickering unnaturally.

'Thought so!' yelled the Doctor. Swinging precariously by one arm again, he quickly pulled out his sonic screwdriver. He aimed it at the right-hand tower dome. A thin, metre-long bolt of green light suddenly shot from its tip.

As the energy pulse struck it, the flickering shape that Amy had made out solidified into a hideous, multi-limbed body. The adult Vispic that was clinging to the dome became fully visible – almost highlighted, in fact, as its entire alien body turned bright orange.

'I've calculated a frequency that messes up their skin-pigment control,' the Doctor shouted down. 'Fixes it temporarily in one tone. At least I can see what I'm dealing with!'

He twisted his arm to turn his dangling body by a hundred and eighty degrees.

'And unless I'm much mistaken . . .'

He took aim and fired off another sonic pulse in the direction of the other tower dome. A moment later, the hulking body of a second adult Vispic became clearly visible, crouching atop the dome. This time, its skin colour had been locked in a shocking pink all over.

The creatures lurking on the twin towers were the size of the smaller adult Vispics Amy and the Doctor had met earlier. These two had come after the Doctor just as the larger adult had come after Amy. It looked likely that the Vispics had figured out that Amy and the Doctor were planning something and were out to stop them.

The Doctor's situation didn't look good. He was now hanging from the wire between the two flagpoles, with a hungry Vispic lying in wait for him at each end. He was left with nowhere to go.

Amy saw the dangling Doctor look from one Vispic to the other, then down at her.

'Wish me luck, Pond!' he yelled. 'Because as much as I'd love to hang around –'

Amy let out a shriek of horror as the Doctor released his grip on the wire and fell.

'DOCTOR!'

The Doctor's body plummeted to the stadium roof, dropping out of Amy's field of vision. She stared at the point where he had vanished, waiting and hoping for a sign that he was okay.

Several seconds passed. Nothing.

Then suddenly Amy saw the Doctor's wild-haired head poke out from over the edge of the roof. He was grinning playfully. 'Did you miss me?'

Amy, craning her neck, gave him an exasperated look. She saw his smile vanish at the sound of two heavy crashes. The Vispics had jumped down from their tower perches to join him on the stadium roof.

'No need to panic!' the Doctor yelled down. 'They'll be displaced as soon as we connect the power!' His right hand appeared over the edge of the roof. It was clutching a coil of electrical cable – the old-fashioned black-and-white fabric-covered kind.

'I'm going to throw this down, Pond! Just clamp the connector to the end and switch it on!'

'Is that going to take a thousand volts, Doctor?' From where Amy was standing, the cable didn't look particularly heavy-duty.

'I've tweaked the core!' yelled back the Doctor. 'It's super-conductive now. It'll be fine. Ready?'

Before Amy could reply, there was an anxious shout from PC Sanderson.

'Agent Beckham!'

Amy turned to see what the problem was.

The third adult Vispic – the largest one – was clattering towards them along Olympic Way. It looked more bizarre than ever. Its camouflage seemed to be only partly working. Bits of its body were clearly visible, while other parts still matched themselves to their background, giving the overall impression of a grotesque, moth-eaten monster.

Amy guessed that the double shocks she had given the Vispic back at the Tube station had taken their toll on the creature's camouflage. Or maybe it was just mad enough not to care whether they could see it or not. Either way, it was still perfectly capable of making a meal out of her and Sanderson.

They needed to make that connection, fast.

Amy turned back to look up at the Doctor on the rooftop. 'Ready, Doctor! Lob it down!'

The Doctor let the cable drop. It uncoiled down the stadium wall as it fell. Amy put her arms out to catch its free end.

But it didn't reach her. Not even close.

Even as it dangled at full length down the face of the wall, its end hung a good seven or eight metres from the ground.

The cable was too short.

Chapter 19

The Dying Seconds

If the final whistle didn't come soon, Rory was going to keel over. He wasn't sure which was more unbearable – the effect of the shimmer on his poor, aching body or the atmosphere of raw, nervous tension that now filled the Empire Stadium.

West Germany had clearly decided that they had nothing to lose. There were only a few minutes of the second period of extra time left to play and they were still a goal down. They were throwing everyone forward in a last-ditch attempt to save the match.

The English fans in the crowd were watching the dying seconds in a frenzy of nervous anticipation. Victory had already been snatched from the English once, only half an hour earlier. They wouldn't dare believe this match was won until it was over.

Rory knew that he shouldn't be sharing their

anxiety – after all, he knew how the match would turn out. Or, at least, he knew how it was meant to turn out. Somehow, his nerves were on a knife-edge, too; it would still only take one moment of German skill to change the scoreline to 3–3.

But there was nothing more Rory could do. He had done his bit. Or, to be more accurate, he had done Bahramov's bit. Surely history must be back on track now.

He watched anxiously as the West German players pressed forward again. There was a tremendous roar from the crowd as Ray Wilson bravely slid in to steal the ball. The English fans were cheering every tackle now.

Rory checked his watch yet again. They were into injury time. England just had to keep hold of the ball . . .

But, moments later, the West Germans had won possession once more. Beckenbauer began a dangerous, weaving run into the English half.

'Come on!' muttered Rory to himself. 'Blow, ref. Blow!'

Outside the stadium, the situation was equally tense.

As soon as it had become obvious that the Doctor's cable was not going to reach her, Amy had resolved to find a way to reach it.

Climbing was not her greatest strength at the best of times; climbing the sheer face of a large building, which offered few handholds or footholds, was proving a real challenge. A very painful, very scary challenge.

She had now made it nearly six metres up the stadium's wall. She was clinging on for dear life, with one hand and both feet somehow maintaining their purchase on the slightest of holds, while she felt about desperately above her for another ridge or ledge by which to pull herself up. She had the crocodile-clip connector clamped firmly between her teeth.

The exposed end of the cable dangled tantalisingly close overhead. It was only a metre or so out of her reach.

Amy could feel the strength ebbing from her arms. The view of the drop to the concrete below made her feel light-headed. She felt sure she would lose her grip at any moment . . . but she had to keep going. All she had to do was get to the cable and make the connection. Just a few more centimetres . . .

On the ground below, PC Sanderson was showing similar bravery in the face of danger. By now, the largest of the adult Vispics – the one that Amy had fought off at the Tube station – would have overcome both of them, were it not for the policeman's desperate actions.

As the Vispic came scuttling into the stadium's forecourt from Olympic Way, Sanderson had leapt back on to his faithful Thunderbird and kick-started the bike's powerful engine. With little thought for his own safety, he had driven the bike straight at the charging Vispic. He was determined to keep the alien beast from harming Amy at all costs.

His headlong motorcycle charge had worked. The Vispic was forced to throw itself to one side to avoid a collision. It came to a halt, then began to scuttle first one way, then the other, weighing up its reckless opponent.

The two were now engaged in a one-on-one stand-off, like the world's most bizarre bullfight. Man and machine against alien monster.

Meanwhile, up on the stadium roof, the Doctor was being kept fully occupied by the other two adult Vispics. They were having their own pitched battle. It was playing out between the stadium's gleaming twin towers. The Vispics were circling the Doctor menacingly while he brandished his sonic screwdriver like a sword.

It didn't look like a fight the Doctor could win. But so far he had managed to evade each sudden, vicious attack thanks to some well-timed dodging and the odd blast of stinging sonic energy.

Down on the ground, the Vispic began its next charge. Sanderson boldly urged the Thunderbird forward to meet it head on. But this time the alien creature got the better of him. It dipped its ugly hammerhead at the last moment, then threw it back, flipping the front wheel of the police bike into the air. Sanderson lost control of it completely. He was thrown from the Thunderbird's saddle. His body hit the forecourt, skidded across it a considerable distance, then lay still. His motorcycle screeched to a standstill on its side some distance away.

The Vispic had no further interest in Sanderson for now. It clearly understood what Amy was attempting to do – and it was intent on stopping her. It scuttled to the base of the wall she was clinging to and began to climb.

To Amy's great dismay, it seemed Vispic leeches made better climbers than girls from Leadworth. Only moments later, she felt an alien claw clutch at her trailing leg. She risked losing her grip by kicking down hard with one foot and landed a solid blow on the Vispic's head. A moment or two later she had the satisfaction of hearing the creature hit the ground below with a clatter.

Amy frantically scrabbled to regain her foothold, then peered down anxiously.

The Vispic was already beginning to climb the wall again.

Bobby Moore, the England captain, won the ball deep in his own half. He looked up and, in a typically inspired moment, spotted the perfect pass to play. The desperate West Germans had pushed up so far, they had left themselves wide open to a fast counter-attack. Moore picked out Geoff Hurst in space on the left wing and sent a gloriously well-judged ball into his teammate's path.

From the touchline, Rory watched Hurst collect Moore's pass and begin streaking upfield with the ball. As Hurst did so, all sense of anxiety lifted from Rory. Once again, he recognised this moment – he had relived it on YouTube countless times, and it never lost its ability to fascinate and thrill him. What was about to happen, Rory knew, was the greatest moment in English football history.

'Go on, Geoff! GO ON!' Rory cheered wildly as the English centre-forward ran past him, the ball at his feet. Rory didn't care any more that he was supposed to be Russian, or Azerbaijani, or whatever. Nor did he care that, right at that moment, he had the most terrible stomach ache of his entire life.

All he cared about was what was about to happen.

After almost two hours of full-on football, Hurst somehow found the energy to sprint the entire length of the pitch. He took the ball past the final German outfield player. As he bore down on the German goal from the left wing, he drilled a powerful left-footed, long-range shot towards the near top corner of the net . . .

With one final heroic heave, Amy pulled herself up to within reach of the dangling cable. She let go of the wall with her right hand, risking a deadly fall, and pulled the connector from her mouth. She stretched the fingers of her right hand to their limit to grasp both its handles and squeezed them together.

Something cold and sharp scraped against the back of her right leg.

She desperately raised the connector until its jaws were round the exposed cable end, clamped it on and gave the red handle a firm twist.

One thousand volts of electricity instantly surged along the cable. They flowed into the complex inverter-transformer circuit that the Doctor had ingeniously engineered from Wembley's vast aluminium roof structure. The voltage was boosted a hundredfold, before the pulse finally shot up the flagpole of the left-hand stadium tower and along the wire that connected it to the other pole.

The displacement anchor, secured at the midpoint of the wire, glowed brilliantly, blindingly white for an instant.

Then it exploded into a million tiny pieces, like a puff of glittering powder.

All three adult Vispics vanished in the blink of an eye. Amy, the Doctor and PC Sanderson, who had now struggled back to his feet, found themselves alone.

And all along the north-west branch of the Metropolitan Line, bewildered Tube drivers wondered why their trains had just ground to a halt.

Amy wasn't out of danger yet, though. The last drop of strength in her left-hand fingertips was draining away fast. She couldn't hold on much longer. With one last exertion, she twisted back the red connector handle to kill the power. Then she scrabbled at the wall hopelessly with her right hand. But there was nothing to grip on to.

Her left foot slipped, and she fell.

A split second later, she found herself dangling in thin air – not falling through it. Something was clinging to her right wrist. A hand.

'Gotcha!'

Amy looked up into the anxious face of the Doctor. Much of it was covered by his drooping hair, which had flopped forward due to the fact that he was hanging almost upside down. Somehow, he had managed to drop from the stadium roof and slide down the power cable in time to catch her.

'Nice work, Agent Beckham!' Despite the effort he was clearly putting into keeping hold of her, the Doctor forced a smile. 'Never doubted for a moment that you had things under control!'

Amy looked up at him, her pale face paler than ever. 'Did we do it, Doctor?' she asked. 'Are they gone? Do you think it's all over?'

At that moment, a deafening roar rose from inside the stadium – the roar of tens of thousands of rejoicing spectators. Hurst had scored his third goal. The match was over. England had beaten West Germany, four goals to two.

And, under the South Stand, not a single luck-sucking larva remained to feast on the elation of the euphoric England fans.

As the Doctor replied to Amy, his grin broadened. 'It is now!'

Epilogue

The Doctor, Amy and Rory turned off Olympic Way and strolled eastward along Fulton Road.

The city streets were very different from the last time Amy had made this journey. The pavements were now packed with celebrating England supporters. Some had spilled out from the stadium itself; others were Londoners who had left their homes to join the party. They were all chanting, singing, waving their Union Jacks or simply clinging to one another in sheer delight.

As the three friends crossed the street, they had to hurry out of the path of a human snake of whooping revellers dancing the conga – 'Dada-da-da-da-DAH!' – along the centre of the road.

Despite the party atmosphere, Amy felt a little weary to be making this particular trek again.

'I still don't see why you couldn't let Bill give me a lift,' she grumbled. She had enjoyed riding pillion on the young police officer's patrol bike. It would have been even more pleasant without a pursuing alien.

'He has better things to do, Pond,' said the Doctor. 'Good man, that Sanderson. I thought we could trust him to tidy up a few loose ends.'

In fact, the Doctor – in his role as Agent Lineker – had assigned the helpful constable a number of important tasks before they parted company back at the stadium. Sanderson was to check on the condition of the unconscious Bahramov and, when the linesman revived, order him not to say a word about his peculiar experience. He was also to recover the body of the Vispics' victim – the man they had found in the changing room – and ensure that his death was put down to natural causes, so as to prevent unnecessary alarm. Finally, he was to keep this entire Code Thirteen affair secret – for reasons of national security, of course.

The Doctor had made it very clear that he and Agent Beckham – and indeed the entire population of London – owed PC Sanderson a great debt of thanks. Special Branch would watch his career with interest.

'Aww! It's shut!' complained Rory. They were approaching Syd Marlin's news stand once again, where the Doctor had bought his paper earlier. 'I was gonna get a few more of those player stickers.'

'Ooh, wait a second!' The Doctor came to a halt, and began rooting about in his pockets. He pulled out several coins. Although the news stand was closed, there was a narrow gap under its shutters. The Doctor poked several of the larger coins through this gap.

'Just a few shillings, or florins, or groats, or whatever they are, in case I didn't pay that chap enough . . .'

They set off along the pavement again. A group of happy fans hailed them from the other side of the road. The young men whirled their football rattles. Over the loud *tatta-tatta-tatta* sound, they began a rousing chorus of 'Rule, Britannia!'

Rory was carrying a rattle of his own. He had told Amy, when they had eventually managed to regroup after the match, that he had found it and decided to keep hold of it as a souvenir.

Rory was in particularly high spirits. England had just become world champions, after all. And it was a huge relief to have removed the shimmer at last. Rory couldn't describe how good it was to feel – and look – like himself again. No more dodgy tummy and daft tash.

His only regret was that neither Amy nor the Doctor had seen his moment of glory. They didn't seem to have caught any of the match, in fact. When

Rory had asked Amy why not, she had just snapped that they had been 'a little bit busy'.

Rory saluted the singing fans with an enthusiastic whirl of his own wooden rattle. He saw Amy wince at the noise it made.

'What?' Rory gave her a hurt look. 'Aw, come on, Amy! I just single-handedly rescued England's World Cup victory. I deserve something to remember it by, don't I?'

Amy didn't answer. Instead, she changed the subject. 'Speaking of remembering, you two haven't forgotten our deal, right?' She gave both Rory and the Doctor a steely look. 'About where we're taking the TARDIS next? I only agreed to come here on the condition that we go straight on to see the final when Scotland wins, remember?'

'Yes, Pond,' said the Doctor. 'We recall.'

'Good. So long as that's understood, boys.'

'You're absolutely sure the Scots do win it sometime, Doctor?' Rory clearly found this hard to swallow. 'I mean, the actual World Cup?'

Amy came to an abrupt halt. She confronted Rory, hands on hips. 'And why shouldn't they?'

There was danger in Amy's fiery glare.

Rory opened his mouth to reply, but the Doctor cut in before things turned nasty. 'I guarantee, Rory, that Scotland are future world champions,' he said quickly. 'As you will both duly see for yourselves.'

Amy gave Rory a fierce 'so there' look, then strode off along the pavement again.

'Though we are talking about the very, very far-off future-y future,' the Doctor added, in a whispered aside to Rory. Rory grinned at him. They set off after Amy.

'Anyway, another football outing is cool by me,' said Rory, as they caught up with her. 'But this time I'm *not* getting involved. Strictly spectating. *Come . . . on . . . you . . . blues!*'

As he practised his supporter's chant, he gave his wooden rattle another enthusiastic whirl.

Tatta-tatta-tatta!

Without warning, Amy snatched the rattle from Rory's grasp. Before he could stop her, she stepped off the pavement, held it over a storm drain and let it drop. The rattle vanished down a gap in the drain's grating.

'Amy!' Rory was devastated. 'What did you do that for?'

Amy simply brushed off her hands theatrically.

Once again, the Doctor stepped in as peacekeeper.

'Never mind, Rory,' he said briskly. 'Between you and me, I've got an idea for a *much* better World Cup memento. Less noisy, too.'

Rory continued to sulk.

'It would, however, involve us making a very brief stop-off on the way to the Scotland final,' the Doctor told Amy. 'How do you feel about a quick detour to Rio de Janeiro?'

'Brazil?' Amy frowned. 'What for?'

'The headquarters of the Brazilian Football Confederation, to be precise,' the Doctor continued, evading Amy's question. 'The nineteenth of December 1983. Around midnight, shall we say?'

Now Rory couldn't help being intrigued.

'I know that date,' he said. 'That's when the Jules Rimet Trophy got stolen for the second time.' His eyes widened. 'You don't mean . . . ? What, that *we* could . . . ?'

The Doctor grinned mischievously. 'Better than petty thieves having it, don't you think?'

Rory beamed from ear to ear. The World Cup itself. As a souvenir. Wicked.

Amy reached a junction and turned left, leading the others round the corner. They were back on Albion Way, where they had first arrived. There were the two dark blue police call boxes, side by side.

Amy hesitated for a moment.

'There you are, old girl!' The Doctor strode eagerly towards the left-hand box. Rory and Amy followed.

The three of them halted in front of the TARDIS. The Doctor surveyed his faithful craft with an affectionate gaze.

'There's no mistaking the real McCain, eh, you two?'

'It's McCoy, Doctor,' said Rory.

His words fell on deaf ears.

'Still stands out from the crowd, doesn't she?' the Doctor went on proudly.

'Absolutely,' agreed Amy. She looked a little shifty. 'Oh, yeah. Unique.'

A sudden burst of raucous singing caused the three friends to look back towards Fulton Road. They watched another conga line of jubilant England fans dance their way across the end of the street.

'They certainly do love their football, the English, don't they?' said the Doctor. 'I can remember them going just as crazy next time they win it.'

He smiled, then turned his attention back to the TARDIS's doors.

It took Rory's brain a moment to register what the Doctor had just said.

'Next time?' He looked puzzled. Then an expression of pure elation slowly spread across his face. Of all the thousands of football facts stashed in Rory's head, not one was as exciting as this revelation.

'So – England do win the World Cup again?

Yesss!' He did a little victory spin on one heel. 'I *knew* we could! When?'

But the Doctor and Amy were no longer beside him. They had already disappeared into the TARDIS.

'Doctor? When?' Rory hurried after them, closing the door behind him.

The End

Titles in the series:

The Galactic Fair has arrived on the mining asteroid of Stanalan and anticipation is building around the construction of the fair's most popular attraction – the Death Ride! But there is something sinister going on behind all the fun of the fair: people are mysteriously dying in the Off-Limits tunnels. Join the Doctor, Amy and Rory as they investigate . . .

The Doctor finds himself trapped in the virtual world of Parallife. As the Doctor tries to save the inhabitants from being destroyed by a deadly virus, Amy and Rory must fight to keep his body in the real world, safe from the mysterious entity known as Legacy . . .

The Doctor, Amy and Rory are surprised to discover lumps of moon rock scattered around a farm. But things get even stranger when they find out where the moon rock is coming from – a Rock Man is turning everything he touches to stone! Can the Doctor, Amy and Rory find out what the creature wants before it's too late?

The Eleventh Doctor and his friends,
Amy and Rory, join a group of explorers on a
Victorian tramp steamer in the Florida Everglades.
The mysterious explorers are searching for
the Fountain of Youth, but neither they —
nor the treasure they seek — are
quite what they seem . . .

Terrible tiny creatures swarm down from
the sky, intent on destroying everything on planet
Xirrinda. As the colonists try to fight the alien
infestation, the Eleventh Doctor searches for
the ancient secret weapon of the native
Ulla people. Is it enough to save the day?

A distress signal calls the TARDIS to the *Black
Horizon*, a spaceship under attack from the
Empire of Eternal Victory. But the robotic
scavengers are the least of the Eleventh
Doctor's worries. Something terrifying is
waiting to trap him in space . . .

The Eleventh Doctor treats Rory to a trip to the Wild West, where the TARDIS crew find a town full of sleeping people and a gang of menacing outlaws intent on robbing the local bank. But it soon becomes clear that Amy, Rory and the Doctor are not the only visitors to Mason City, Nevada . . .

An ancient artefact awakes, trapping one of the Eleventh Doctor's companions on an archaeological dig in Egypt. The only way for the Doctor to save his friend is to travel thousands of years back in time to defeat the mysterious Water Thief . . .

People are mysteriously disappearing on Moonbase Laika. They eventually return, but with strange bite marks on their bodies and no idea where they have been. Can the Eleventh Doctor get to the bottom of what's going on?

The Eleventh Doctor and his friends head to the 1966 World Cup final. While the Doctor and Amy discover that the Time Lord isn't the only alien visiting Wembley Stadium, Rory finds himself playing a crucial role in this historic England versus West Germany football match . . .

The TARDIS crew are quarantined in Terminal 4000, where the hideous Desponds have destroyed the hopes of all waiting passengers. Can the Eleventh Doctor and his friends save the day by helping everyone to escape, without succumbing to despair themselves?

The Eleventh Doctor and his companions are on board the *Cosmic Rover*, a spaceship orbiting the water-planet Hydron. Joining the crew, they journey underwater on a scientific exploration. But nothing is as it seems on the high-tech submarine. When a virus infects the crew, the Doctor discovers the ship is hiding a dangerous secret . . .

Your story starts here . . .

Do you **love books** and **discovering new stories**? Then **www.puffin.co.uk** is the place for you . . .

- Thrilling adventures, fantastic fiction and laugh-out-loud fun

- Brilliant videos featuring your favourite authors and characters

- Exciting competitions, news, activities, the Puffin blog and SO MUCH more . . .

www.puffin.co.uk